AWAKEN THE DEMON

BY

SHIELA STEWART

The Demon Series – Book One

Decadent Publishing
www.decadentpublishing.com

This book is a work of fiction. Names, characters, places, and incidents are the products of the author's imagination or used fictitiously. Any resemblance to actual events, locales or persons, living or dead, is entirely coincidental.

Awaken the Demon
Copyright 2011 by Shiela Stewart
ISBN: 978-1-61333-097-5
Cover design by Dara England and Cribley Designs

Published by Decadent Publishing Company

Look for us online at:
www.decadentpublishing.com

Printed in the United States of America

"What the Critics are saying...."

Have you ever read a book and when you get to the end think, "what? It's over already? I need more!" Awaken the Demon was that book for me today. Missy Green has stared death in the face, in the form of her fiancé, Ronald. When she flees, she finds a bus full of people called the Starr Gazers. They had been personally invited to Draco Starr's palatial home, in order to study the stars. Draco, for his part, is auditioning humans to see if one of the females is his mate. Quite by accident, Missy finds out that she is part demon and has powers that she can't even begin to imagine. Of course, she doesn't take the news well; but eventually, she comes to grips with her new reality. The best part of the book was watching the suave, debonair Draco fumble a bit with how to deal with his woman. For all intents and purposes, Missy is his first relationship and he doesn't have all the answers, which was awesome. I am definitely looking forward to the next book. ~
Night Owl Reviews

This book really took me by surprise. It was a story of demons, and it is a side of demon we usually don't get to hear about. Usually we read about the nasty side of them, killing everything in its path, turning others into demons or eating them for their raw fleshy meat and blood. This is a unique story of a demon who just wants to be loved and not be lonely anymore. Joanne has no idea she is really a half demon half witch, and all hell breaks loose when she discovers it. Draco and Joanne's chemistry together is one I will not soon forget. I love the humor the story has and it made me chuckle and laugh out loud. I loved the hot sex that finally erupted between them and the suspense that played out while Joanne figured out who she really was and then learning how to use her new found powers. I also loved the compassion Draco had with Joanne when she revealed her true identity and why she had to escape her fiancé. This book I could absolutely not put down once I started and I hope you all enjoy it as much as I did. ~ **Siren Song Reviews**

~DEDICATION~

To my love, William.
I wished upon a falling star and I was given you.
My friend, my love, my life!

CHAPTER ONE

The blade cut through her skin, inducing a searing pain that blurred her vision. He sat on her chest, pinning her arms to her sides with his legs, and looked down at her with deadly intent. She knew this time she would not walk away; this time he would end her life, once and for all.

A small part of her wanted it to stop, and finally put an end to the torment she had endured for the better part of four years. That tiny voice deep within cried out: *fight.*

Struggling to break free, she hit her head on the bottom of the refrigerator, which dazed her. She saw the vase of flowers right before it crashed down on his head. He fell over her, the weight of his body holding her down. The knife slid from her throat, clattering on the tiled kitchen floor beneath them. Momentarily stunned, she lay there listening to his breath as it whispered against her ear.

The pain in her neck reminded her that she had nearly lost her life, and her survival instincts kicked in.

She needed to run!

"Oh, God!" Her hands shaking, she touched his shoulders and carefully slid him away. When his body fell with a thud to her left, she held her breath, fearful he would wake. Quickly, she scurried away, bumping into the cupboard beside her.

Curling her legs up to her chest, eyes wide, body trembling, she stared at Ronald's unconscious body. Just like a deer caught in headlights, she was temporarily frozen.

He moaned, and she scrambled to her feet. Her mind clicked back into gear and she knew she had to run, now, if she ever wanted to see another day.

Rushing up the stairs to her room, Joanne grabbed the backpack she had hidden in the corner of the closet, already packed and ready for this very moment. She'd been planning to leave for months, but never had the nerve to carry through with it.

Until now.

Feeling something warm slide down her neck, she wiped at it with her hand, and saw the bright red blood. Her hands quivering, she looked up and saw her reflection in the mirror. "Oh...God." She quivered, stumbling back. There was so much blood.

Ronald had begun cutting her for thrills just after they'd become engaged, and not a day went by that she didn't suffer at his hands.

"Joanne!"

She jumped at the sound of his voice echoing up the stairs and spun around in a desperate need to escape. There was only one door leading from their room, and she could hear him stumbling up the stairs. She had nowhere to run.

"Joanne!" he bellowed.

"No...no...no..." she repeated, shaking her hands as if that would help her think faster.

"You are going to pay for that, you *bitch*."

She spun around, saw the window. It was her only means of escape. Slinging the backpack over her shoulder, she ran for the window and threw it open. He was getting closer, she could tell by the sound of his voice.

"You think you can hide from me? I know this place like I know the back of my hand. You can't hide from me."

She slid one leg through the window, bracing herself on the

ledge. Her foot slipped and she cried out in fear as she clung to the ledge. The willow tree outside was too far away, and she knew if she tried to reach it, she would only end up falling.

"You can't run from me," his voice slurred from the alcohol he'd indulged in earlier. "You're mine. Mine!" he screamed, moving closer to the window.

She looked down. If she didn't let herself go, he would drag her through the window and back into the house. He would finish the job he had started. He would kill her.

Closing her eyes tight, inhaling deeply, she released her hold and let herself fall. "Don't let me die," she pleaded, as she dropped the two stories to the ground. Her feet hit with a hard thud, her knees buckling. A sharp stabbing sensation shot from her ankles up to her thighs, and she cried out in pain.

"You stupid cunt," he called out through the open window. "You can't even escape properly. Probably broke your legs. God, you're so stupid."

The words echoed in her head, ricocheting off the memories of all the times he had called her those names before. Gathering her strength, she got to her knees, breathing through the pain as she made it to her feet. *Run*, she told herself, and sprinted off despite the burning in her legs.

She heard him screaming at her as she ran, and it was incentive enough to push past the pain to escape.

"You can't get away from me. I'll find you!"

The streets were dark and nearly empty. She ran without stopping. Her life depended on it.

It was a hot summer evening, and the sky showed no indication of cooling down with rain. Her hair clung to her face, damp with sweat. The houses she ran past were only a blur. In the distance, someone's music was blasting through an open window, the song unrecognizable. Her legs burned, but she knew if she slowed down now, Ronald would still have time to catch her. Swallowing her pain, she turned the corner and nearly ran someone down in the process.

"Whoa there, missy. What's the rush?"

Panicked, her heart pounding so hard she felt ill from it, she continued to run.

Where was she going to go? What was she going to do? He would find her, and he would drag her home, and kill her.

I don't want to dieI don't want to die.

The blood from her wound trickled down her neck. Ducking behind a building, she opened her backpack to look for her jacket. Though it was a warm June evening, it was her only choice until she could get somewhere to clean and bandage the wound. Slipping on the heavy fall jacket, she zipped it right to her chin, and slung the pack over her shoulder. With a quick peak around the building, she darted out, and continued hurrying away, keeping her head down so as not to be recognized.

She heard a car pull up beside her and as she turned, saw Ronald behind the wheel.

"Get in the fucking car, Jo!"

Joanne screamed and bolted off. She ran down the street and slipped into an alley. When she heard his tires squealing, she knew he was coming after her. At the end, she turned left and continued to run. The sound of voices ahead drew her attention. As she looked up, she saw the crowd. Maybe she could lose him there. Pushing herself, she ran faster. As she neared the throng of people, she slowed down. Slipping into the crowd, she mingled while keeping watch for Ronald's car.

When a hand clamped onto her arm, Joanne nearly screamed. Lifting her head, she saw a chubby-faced brunette, and mercifully, not her fiancé.

"We're about to board. Whoa, cool tinted contacts. C'mon. You can sit with me."

"What?" Confused, she looked around at the crowd before her.

"Your eyes. I like the colored contacts. The gold goes well with your black hair."

"They're not contacts."

"Really? Weird. Come on, we're boarding."

Baffled, she found herself tugged toward the crowd. "No, I...I don't—"

"Is that all you've got?"

"Pardon me?"

"Personal belongings. You just have the one bag?"

"Yes." Before she could protest, the woman pulled her forward, and when she looked up, she saw a big black bus before her. "What's going on?"

"We're about to board. Isn't this exciting? I'm Jennifer Laurence, by the by. And you are?"

Board a bus? Her first thought was to break free and continue running, until she heard a car squeal to a stop. Looking in the direction of the sound, she saw Ronald climb out of the car. She couldn't let him find her.

"Hey, hello." The woman snapped her fingers in front of her face, startling her. "You okay?"

She was anything but okay. "Yes."

"What's your name?"

Keeping an eye on Ronald, she inched closer to the woman. Using her real name was not an option, not if she wanted to get away from Ronald. "Missy." The name just popped into her head. That's what he'd called her, that man she'd nearly knocked down a minute ago.

"Missy what?"

"Green. Missy...Green." All she could think of was her favorite color. It was a decent name, she supposed.

"Cool. Well, looks like it's our turn. Come on."

Seeing the open door ahead, Joanne slid in between two other people and Jennifer and inched her way onto the bus. She hoped no one asked her for a ticket or money because she had neither. Jennifer's hand clamped around her arm again and jerked her into a seat near the back. She had no idea where she was going, let alone what she would find when she got there.

"Just think, Missy, in a few hours, we are going to meet with the creator of the Starr Gazers foundation, and spend the next three weeks learning about the constellations."

I don't want to die.

Missy. The name sounded so strange. It was something she was going to have to get used to, quickly.

"Missy?"

"Oh...um...yeah." She had no idea what Jennifer was talking about. Star-gazers or something. She lifted her eyebrows. She'd always loved looking at the stars, so it might be an interesting adventure. She gripped the seat in front of her as the bus began to roll. There was no getting off now.

"Looks like we're off and running. I can't wait to go to Erie. Three weeks of living in a mansion, not having to cook or clean for ourselves. No parents to nag at you. No boss bitching at you because you showed up late, again. And all we have to do is watch some stars, take a quiz or two, and possibly get a job. Piece of cake."

Erie? That was far enough away from Middletown that Ronald wouldn't come looking for her. Sitting back in her seat, she gave the idea some serious thought. Maybe this was a blessing. Even if she didn't know where she was going, exactly, she was getting away from Ronald. She had a new name, and was now making a fresh start.

Looking out the window, through the darkness, she watched Ronald frantically search for her.

She had survived, and was finally free. Maybe her luck was changing. Someone was looking out for her after all.

Slipping the engagement ring from her finger, she pressed it into the fold of the seat. She never wanted to see it again.

She closed her eyes and drifted off to sleep.

"Wake up, lazybones. We're here."

Missy's eyes shot open. The hand on her arm brought fear sharp into her mind. "I'm awake, I'll start breakfast."

"Um, I don't think you'll need to do that. We're here," she

repeated as Missy looked around frantically.

"Oh." A wave of relief washed over her when she got her bearings. The bus had stopped but she was clueless as to where they were.

"Let's go."

Missy only had a moment to compose herself when Jennifer hoisted her up with one quick jerk and pulled her along. When she stepped from the bus, she stood in awe. It was sunrise and a glorious one at that. The cloudless combination of blues and orange beckoned to her. Here is your peace, it seemed to say.

A new day and beginning.

She saw the mansion ahead and all thought vanished but the beauty of the house. It reminded her of an old-world castle she had seen in a magazine once. It was tall, regal, and stunning. Vines climbed from the ground to the middle of the building, reaching, she thought, to the sun. Tiny purple flowers sneaked in through the green foliage. French windows gleamed. She had no doubt the help cleaned them every day. The building was a remarkable sight to behold, all brick and stone and incredible-looking.

"Holy shit!" Jennifer gaped, wide-mouthed, as she stared at the house.

"And then some." Missy craned her neck to get a look at the top of the mansion. How many rooms did it have, she wondered?

"Hi, I'm Lou." A tall, dark-haired young man approached them with extended hand and a bright smile.

Missy tore her eyes from the castle and smiled back as she took his hand. "Hi Lou, I'm...Missy."

"I'm Jennifer."

He turned his head and simply smiled at Jennifer.

"I'm Deb, and this is my boyfriend Troy." A small-framed, blonde-haired woman introduced herself. She clung possessively to a handsome young man with long sandy hair that waved all the way down to rest on the tops of his shoulders.

"Nice to meet you." Troy took Missy's hand in his, and held it a bit too long for her comfort while his eyes probed into hers.

Something in his flashy smile told her to be wary. "Nice to meet both of you."

"I'm one of the group leaders. If you have any questions, don't be afraid to ask." His voice was low and husky and his eyes twinkled with intent.

Oh yeah, she had best be very wary about this one. "Thank you, Troy. I'll keep that in mind." That was, if she had any intentions of sticking around, which she didn't. The first chance she got, she was going to make a break for it.

"If I could have everyone split into two lines, we'll get to marking you off the list of attendees," Lou stated as he stepped off to the side. "Let's try and make it even."

Darn it! Missy looked around, trying to figure out a getaway before someone realized she didn't belong. Breaking free of Jennifer, she darted around the bus. The only road out was directly in view of where both Lou and Troy were facing. She'd just have to wait until everyone was finished and head inside. Her heart pounding in her chest, she listened as they called out names. It seemed to take forever. When she heard Jennifer's name, she breathed a sigh of relief. Closing her eyes, Missy waited.

"There you are."

Her eyes shot open to the sight of Jennifer beaming at her.

"What are you doing over here?"

"I...uh...dropped something by the bus."

"Oh, well. Did they call your name already?"

Now what? "Yes," she lied.

"Great! Come on, then." Jennifer grabbed her arm and once again dragged her along.

As they entered the grand wooden front doors, Missy gaped at what she saw on the inside. *My oh my, what a house.* The entrance was like a hotel lobby, but far more sophisticated and glamorously decorated. A tall, three-tiered crystal chandelier hung overhead and twinkled bright. The floor beneath her feet was black marble, and shiny enough that she could see her reflection. Before her was the grandest staircase she had ever seen. The steps were also in black marble and wound in a spiral to the second floor. Whoever owned this place had money, and liked to show it off.

"My name is Hunter and I'll be at your service while you stay with Mr. Starr. Anyone wishing to freshen up before we eat may do so in the guest washrooms just down the hall." The middle-aged gentleman wearing a dark brown suit, perfectly pressed, pointed a long boney finger down the hall.

"Let's go."

Missy was really beginning to hate the way Jennifer tugged her along like a puppy on a leash. She wished just once the girl would let her be so she could make her escape. Before she had a chance to break free, Jennifer shoved her into the washroom.

"Oh, wow!" Jennifer stopped and was, for a moment at least, silent.

"Indeed." Missy was astounded at the pureness of the large, bright washroom. It was so white and clean, it looked as though no one had used it before.

"I figure a person that lives like this has to be incredibly happy."

"Money doesn't buy happiness."

"I would be willing to find out," Jennifer quipped as she pulled a brush from her purse.

Glancing in the mirror, Missy nearly gasped. Her normally golden skin looked drawn and sickly. Her eyes, eyes that had always fascinated people—gold, with no hint of brown or green, just pure gold—looked tired and worn. Her long wavy jet-black hair looked dull and scraggily. She looked pathetic. She looked like a runaway.

"You need the brush?" Jennifer held it out to her.

Missy turned, took the brush and began running it down the length of her hair. Ronald had stripped away everything that had once been a vibrant beautiful woman, and had left her in a withering heap of shame. It was time to put an end to his control.

"What happened there?" Jennifer touched the bandage on Missy's arm.

She pulled her arm away. "I cut it, accidentally." *You're lying for him, as always.*

"Must be pretty bad for such a large bandage."

"It's fine." She wasn't about to tell the woman her fiancé had sliced it the day before in a fit of rage.

The knock on the door had both their heads turning.

"It's time to head to the dining hall, ladies." Hunter called through the door.

Missy handed Jennifer the brush and started for the door. "Isn't this so cool?"

Missy shrugged. Slipping from the room, she saw the crowd of people waiting in the lobby. No escaping now. Maybe it wouldn't hurt just to stick around for a little while, she decided as she melded with the crowd. What harm would it do?

Hunter led down a long hall to another room, which was obviously the dining hall. Missy could picture opulent dinner parties and dances.

"Can you imagine living here?" Jennifer's voice bubbled as her eyes scanned the suite.

"Hmmm," Missy mumbled as she drank in the room. The walls, painted in deep greens, gave it a mysterious look. Dark mahogany wood framed the walls as well as the doors, and looked fresh and polished. On all the walls, gold-framed pictures of stars hung in abundance. To some, the décor might seem ostentatious, but to Missy it looked magical. She'd had so little delight in her life as of late, and this little piece of beauty gave her a thrill.

"Please, come in and take a seat, everyone," Hunter instructed.

People hurried to the long table set up in the middle of the room. Missy chose a chair near the far end of the table with her back facing the door. Admiring the wealth of food spread out before them, she nearly didn't hear the butler when he spoke.

"Please rise and greet the founder of the Starr Gazers Foundation and the reason you are all here today."

The room became silent. Missy stood quickly and turned to the door.

What she saw astounded her.

CHAPTER TWO

His presence seemed to radiate throughout the room, filling it. He stood tall, broad, and regal. He had short ebony hair, slicked back from a strong-boned and sturdy bronzed face. He wore a black double-breasted suit with a deep silver shirt and black tie. This man radiated class from head to toe, and emitted an authority that all would know upon first sight.

He was handsome, stunningly so, and any woman with a beating heart would be affected, thought Missy. But it was his eyes. Something was off about the eyes. They were large, deep-set, and dark. That was it, they were nearly black. Or was it the light that made them look so dark?

His eyes settled on hers and made her heart jump like a rabbit in her chest.

"Thank you all for coming." He held his hands up, the light catching the stunning gold watch on his wrist, before he lowered his hands slowly.

He didn't walk, she thought, as he moved toward the table. He glided. As he passed by, his scent drifting over her, she felt the breath escape from her lungs. She had seen beautiful men before. Why did this one take her breath away?

She watched him carefully, almost as if her eyes had no will of their own. He stood before a chair she thought was suited for a king: high-backed, bronze, and very ancient. Here was a man who had everything he could possibly want in life, and it showed.

"It is a pleasure to see so many bright faces this early in the morning. I know your trip was tiresome so I won't keep you long. You have all come here today for the same reason. To learn of the stars." He raised his hands, and almost magically the lights dimmed and the ceiling gave way to a glow of twinkling little stars.

Mouths gaping, everyone let out a long gasp.

"You were chosen amongst many to come to my home, a privilege in itself." He lowered his large hands, signaling them all to take a seat before he took his chair.

Missy sat in amazement, watching, listening. His voice held a hint of an accent she couldn't quite figure out. Yugoslavian, or Russian maybe? She wasn't completely sure.

"I hope to get to know each and every one of you personally while you stay here in my home, and I promise all of you that you will not be disappointed. I have the most up-to-date equipment that will allow you to see phenomena you might never have seen before in your life," he continued, his gaze sliding from one person to the next until finally settling on Missy.

She felt an odd sort of heat radiate inside of her, one she had never felt before.

"Some of you might find this to be a turning point. A new change. I hope to be a part of that. Now, let us partake in the feast that was prepared for your arrival."

People grabbed dishes of food and gladly filled their plates. Missy, having waited hours since she ate last, filled hers as well. Her appetite was ravenous and she dug in eagerly to the variety of food she had heaped on her plate. While she ate, she felt his gaze on her, as if he was trying to bore into her brain. Closing her eyes, she told herself to ignore him and the nervousness his stare brought.

"Isn't this just the best thing ever?" Jennifer giggled as she sipped from her water glass.

"What?"

"This place, the founder, isn't it incredible?" Jennifer went on with exuberance.

"It's definitely something." It seemed odd to her, more than anything. The whole thing was odd, including the man who claimed to be the founder. Why would a person get on a bus, head to a place they'd never been before, stay at a home of a complete stranger just for some stars? Moreover, what made a person invite total strangers into his home? Something felt off.

"Isn't he gorgeous? I think I'm in love."

Missy let out a slow sigh. "He gives me the creeps." She glanced over and saw him staring at her once again. She smiled at him, politely, feeling uneasy. "He keeps staring at me."

"How can such a fine specimen of a man give you the creeps?"

Missy turned away from the eyes that seemed to be pulling the air from her lungs. "He just does." She kept her gaze down, making sure to look everywhere but in his direction.

"Girl, you are strange," Jennifer chuckled and turned to the young man seated next to her and struck up a conversation.

Their illustrious host stood and the room fell silent as they all turned to him. "I must take my leave now. Hunter will show you to your rooms when you are done. Rest, refresh, I will see you all later." He moved from his place, gliding past people and pausing only briefly when he reached the end of the table where Missy sat.

Her body tensed. His presence unnerved her, almost as if he were trying to slide inside of her. Shivering, she decided it was best just to ignore him. She let out a long breath when he finally left the room.

"If you all would just follow me, I, along with your guides, will show you to your rooms." Hunter stood by the door, his hands resting at his sides like a proper servant.

"I can't wait," sighed Jennifer. "After that meal, I could use some sleep."

Though she'd slept on the bus, it hadn't been a restful sleep. It might be nice to catch a nap, alone for the first time in a long time.

They followed Hunter up stairs that seemed to keep going, and then down a long hallway. Each person had their own room, which was astounding given the fact that there were at least twenty of them. Why one man needed a home so large with so many rooms was beyond her. Missy was grateful she wouldn't have to room with Jennifer.

When Hunter took her to her suite, Missy stood in awe. The room was incredibly large. It consisted of a sitting room fully furnished with a sofa and chair and a dining area complete with a table and four chairs. Very nice, she thought, as she ran her hands over the soft navy blue fabric. The gleaming wooden table sat near a wide set of French doors that led to a small terrace. Opening the doors, she stared wide-eyed, not only at the size of the terrace, but the beautiful view of the land. The green grass spread out as far as the eye could see. On the terrace, two white cast-iron chairs sat at opposite ends of a small white cast-iron table. A pot of some sort of green leafy plant sat on top. The scene was breathtaking.

Heading back inside, she opened the door she assumed led to the bedroom and stared in amazement at the huge four-poster bed. It had white silk linens with lace-covered pillows and looked like a fluffy cloud. She imagined it would feel the same. In the corner sat a large armoire, and across the room, there was a dressing table with a mirror that looked incredibly expensive. The whole room was like something out of a fairy tale and it made her smile. It had to be at least twice the size of her old room.

She set her bag on the bed, sat down, and had a good cry.

So much had happened to her in the course of one day. She'd run for her life, found a group of people and been swallowed up in the crowd. Now, she sat in a room, in a house belonging to a very strange yet intriguing man, and felt overwhelmed with emotions.

What the hell am I doing here? *I don't belong here. I don't belong anywhere.*

There was no way she was going back, but forward, the future, was so uncertain. With a heavy sigh, Missy wiped her face dry before walking to the adjoining bathroom.

Unzipping her jacket, she peeled back the collar and it tore at the dried blood that coated her skin. Wincing, she eased the fabric away and tossed the jacket on the floor. Her neck needed to be cleaned before it got infected, as did her wrist. Missy hissed when the bandage on her wrist tugged at the wound and the skin.

Running the shower as hot as she could stand it, she stepped inside. The water burned; her wounds stung. She wiped at the cuts with a soft navy cloth while her tears mixed with the hot water. Her skin throbbed a steady drumming beat that could match any of the rock music played on the radio. Missy cried as she scrubbed and cleaned the cut.

She didn't want to think of what she had endured. Didn't want to think of her past and couldn't think to the future. Everything was so uncertain. She should be happy to have made it out alive. Yet, she felt nothing but despair. Sliding to the floor of the tub, curled into a ball. Missy wept endlessly. The hot water rushed over her while her body shook with tears.

Missy felt much more refreshed after her bout of misery, and the tiny nap she had managed to catch. Reluctantly, she left her room when called to dinner, and once again, Jennifer was at her side. She had babbled non-stop about her room, about how cool it was. The woman was always so exuberant.

They sat to a wonderful meal of beef and potatoes, grilled to perfection. Only this time their host hadn't joined them, much to Missy's relief. It was short-lived though. When the announcement came that he would be conducting personal introductions with each member after dinner, she tensed. A private meeting was just what she didn't need.

What was she supposed to tell him? Not the truth, that was for sure. He would most likely call the police. She just wanted to put her past behind her. If she never saw Ronald again it would suit her just fine.

Lying was her best option. After all, she'd convinced her fiancé that she still loved him and that he would be the only man for her, all the while wishing him dead under her breath.

Time had come for her to get away before it was too late.

"Your name, Miss?" Hunter asked, startling Missy.

"M-mmissy Green," she stammered, wetting her dry lips.

He gestured for the door. "Draco wishes to see you first."

She stood from her seat, a trickle of fear nesting inside her gut, and followed him. She had to stay calm. She'd dealt with the worst sort of man, her fiancé. She could certainly deal with this Draco Starr, for pity's sake.

Hunter led her to a pair of tall, deep mahogany wooden doors, swung them open, and stepped inside. "Missy Green to see you, sir."

Mr. Starr stood as handsome and regal as before, and shifted his dark leering eyes to her. "Please, come in." His smile was a flash of warmth.

She had a quick thought to run, but sucked in a breath and walked into the room.

"It's a pleasure to meet you, Missy." He held his out hand to her, the smile still filling his face.

"Nice to meet you, Mr. Starr." As she gripped his hand, the sharp snap of electricity startled her. "Oh my. I'm sorry."

"Not to worry about it. Please, call me Draco."

He surprised her by holding the chair for her as she took a seat.

"So, Missy, tell me about yourself?" He pulled a cigarette from a gold case and casually lit it with a glittering gold lighter, never taking his eyes off her.

Couldn't he have asked her something else, anything else?

She supposed she could give him half-truths. "I'm twenty three, single and eager to learn about the stars."

"Is that all there is to Missy Green? Is Missy short for Melissa?"

"It's just Missy and yes, that's all there is to me." Considering the fact that Missy Green hadn't existed before yesterday, there really wasn't much to tell.

"I see." He leaned back in his leather chair and drew on his cigarette. "There must be more to you than that."

She wished he wouldn't look at her as if she were a luxurious meal he was about to savor. "I've led a dull life."

"How unfortunate. Tell me, just Missy..." His smile was ever-so-charming and made her feel very uneasy. "Why have you decided to join my group?"

Right place, right time, she thought, but that response she kept to herself. "As I said, I want to learn more about stars."

"They are fascinating, and stunning to look at. Do you have family, Missy?"

She watched him crush out the cigarette with his long, slender fingers. She noticed that he wore a ring on the middle finger of his right hand. It was unusual, a solid gold band with an etching that reminded her of snakeskin.

"Yes." There was no point lying about that and what harm would it be to admit she did.

"Are you close with them?" He twined his fingers, rested his elbows on the arms of his chair, and watched her carefully.

"Somewhat." Her thoughts shifted to her father, brothers, and sister. Had Ronald called them yet? What must they think of her now? Would they understand?

"They know of your decision to join my group?"

They weren't aware of anything. "Yes."

"And they have no difficulties with you traveling the world, possibly out of contact for long periods of time?"

"I'm a grown woman. I can take care of myself." She shifted uncomfortably in her chair. His gaze boring into her made her uneasy.

"Headstrong and beautiful. A stunning combination." He smiled at her. "So, Missy is a self-sufficient strong-willed person. And you said there wasn't much to you. I sense there is more to you than meets the eye."

"What you see is what you get, I'm afraid."

"I highly doubt that, but we'll leave it at that for now." He stood, gave his suit jacket a tug, and looked at her intently. "It's been a pleasure speaking with you." His moves were slow and meticulous as he walked around the desk. "Please, feel free to make yourself at home while you are here." He held his hand out to hers.

Standing, Missy took his hand out of the politeness she'd been raised to convey. This man had opened his home to her. She jumped again when there was a snap as their hands connected. "Mercy."

"You seem to be full of energy." He laughed, catching her off guard. "I look forward to seeing more of you." Lifting her hand to his lips, he placed a soft kiss to her knuckles before he released it.

Uneasy with his gesture, she hurried to the door.

Draco rested a hip on the corner of his desk and drew in the scent Missy left behind. A delicate fragrance well suited to her beauty. He felt compelled to find out all there was to know about the intriguing young woman with the golden eyes. He'd never seen anyone with gold eyes before. A birth defect no doubt, but an attractive one nonetheless.

"Shall I send in the next person, sir?" Hunter stood at the door, his hands folded neatly in front of him, his back straight.

"In a moment." Draco lit another cigarette while his mind lingered on the beauty who'd just been in his presence. "I want you to do a search on Missy Green. Find out who she is, where she is from. I want to know everything." His dark eyes turned to Hunter, his loyal and most trusted employee, one who had been with him for more than a hundred years now. "As soon as possible."

"Yes, sir. I'll get right on it."

Draco skirted the desk. "Send in the next person." It would be a difficult task to concentrate on the others, now that Missy took up so much of his mind. However, he had a quest, one he'd had for a long time.

The vision of Missy filled his mind even as her scent faded from the room. It might be interesting to pursue the raven-haired beauty while he searched for the halfling. Only he wouldn't make the mistake Pythos had. Draco was always careful to use protection when with a human. He valued his life too much to give it up over a child.

He closed his eyes a moment, and tucked the picture of Missy safely inside his mind.

CHAPTER THREE

The last thing Missy wanted to do was socialize, yet somehow Jennifer managed to drag her along into the crowd. Apparently, the group had decided to gather in the lounge.

"God, I want to be rich. This is so cool." Jennifer giggled in her frivolous way as she pulled Missy to a table. "Can we join you?"

Turning his head, Troy's eyes instantly fell upon Missy. "With pleasure."

Missy nearly shuddered, but kept it inside as she took a seat. Were all men pigs, or had she just happened to meet the crazy ones? He was openly flirting with her while his arm curled around his girlfriend.

"What can I get you?" the tall, leggy blonde waitress asked as she approached the table.

"Beer, anything on tap will do," Jennifer piped in with exuberance.

"Cola, thank you," Missy stated politely and received a curious look from the waitress before moving on.

"So how did your interview go with Draco, Missy?" Troy asked as he lifted his glass to his lips.

Missy marshaled her thoughts as she watched the waitress return. She waited until they had their drinks before responding. "I assume as well as everyone else's."

"Isn't that just the strangest name? Draco?" Jennifer interrupted, lifting her beer. She downed a quarter of it, then took a breath before speaking. "The accent fits."

"I wouldn't know one accent from another," Deb piped in as she leaned possessively against Troy's arm.

Missy was all too aware of how Troy was looking at her now. She wondered if his girlfriend had any clue. Shifting in her seat, trying not to let it affect her, Missy sipped her drink.

Troy leaned over the table, his eyes deep and seductive. "Why don't you tell us about yourself?"

Missy cleared her throat, twisted her hands around her glass nervously. If anyone knew how she had acquired the name...well, it was best no one ever did. "Not much to tell."

He pulled out a cigarette, offered one to Deb; she declined. "I doubt you're a boring person, Missy." He held the pack out to her; once again his eyes roved seductively. "Smoke?"

Missy shook her head. The guy had some nerve. "I quit years ago." Actually, Ronald had forced her to quit. It was time to stop thinking like that. She was free now and needed to stop dwelling on the past.

He tucked the pack into his pocket then lit his cigarette and kept his eyes on her. "I haven't got the patience or the will to quit."

"Those will kill you," Jennifer preached, before lifting the drink to her lips.

Troy's eyes shifted slowly to Jennifer, his voice turning cool. "So can booze," he countered snidely. "And dozens of other things I don't worry about."

"When I die, I want it to be quick and painless," Deb slurred. She'd obviously had too much to drink already but that didn't stop her from lifting the glass to her lips.

"Same here. I hate pain." Jennifer tipped her empty bottle to the waitress.

"You're awfully quiet, Missy."

"Sorry." *Don't apologize, you fool.* But it would be easier to cut off a finger than to stop something that had been embedded into her, beaten into her for so long.

"No need to apologize. You never got around to telling us about yourself." He drew on his cigarette, letting the smoke linger in his mouth before expelling it into the air.

"There's nothing to tell. I'm afraid I'm rather boring."

"I bet after a couple of drinks you would loosen up," Troy teased as he raised his bottle.

She twisted the glass of cola in her hands. "I don't drink." She'd seen what alcohol could do to a person, had seen it repeatedly in Ronald. It made an already ugly person hideous.

"Get real. Everyone drinks," Deb slurred.

"I'm the exception, I guess." Missy lifted her glass and sipped, her eyes cast down.

"You definitely *are* exceptional."

She looked up at Troy in shock. How could he come on to her so openly, when his girlfriend sat beside him, draped over him?

"You're such a flirt, Troy." Deb giggled in her drunken state, and placed a sloppy kiss to his cheek.

His eyes narrowed on Missy's as he ignored his girlfriend. "When you're good at something, why hide it?"

Missy countered by glaring at him. "Some things are better kept hidden."

"Is that what you're trying to do with that long-sleeved dress and scarf? Avoiding telling us about yourself?" He leaned over the table, his eyes focused on hers. "Hiding something?"

Her heart raced, making her dizzy. Could he tell she had a neck wound? "I'm not trying to hide anything. It's just the way I dress." This was why she never spoke up; it always got her in trouble.

"I need to lay down, Troy. I don't feel so good." Deb swayed as she lifted her dizzy head from Troy's shoulder.

"I'll get you to bed, baby, so you can rest." Shifting his drunken girlfriend, Troy's eyes turned to Missy. "Have a good night."

"Nighty-night." Jennifer waved as they left.

Having had enough socializing for one day, Missy pushed from the table and got to her feet. "I think I'm going to call it a night, too."

"Aw, come on. Stay, the night is young."

"It's been a long day for me. Sleep well, Jennifer." She left before Jennifer could find some way to convince her to stay. All she wanted was some peace, a good night's sleep, alone. What she really didn't want, or need, was to find Troy waiting for her when she reached her door. Yet, there he was.

"Going to bed so soon, Missy?" Troy leaned against his door, his legs crossed at the ankles, an obvious look of intent in his eyes.

Exasperated, wishing he would just leave her alone, Missy didn't even worry about being polite this time. "Yes, I'm rather tired." Opening her door, she caught the movement out of the corner of her eye. Turning, she came face to face with Troy.

"That's too bad. I was hoping we could get to know each other a bit better." He twined a lock of her hair around his fingers.

She pulled her hair free and scowled at him. "Don't you have a girlfriend?"

His smile had the charm of a snake ready to strike. "She's out cold right now and not a lot of fun." He ran his finger along her arm. "I have a feeling you could be a load of fun." His fingers slid up and along her shoulder.

She slapped his hand away, surprising herself for such a bold move. "Good night, Troy." Pushing him aside, she made sure to slam the door in his face. She clicked the lock and let out a long breath. The guy had some nerve, making a play for her when his girlfriend slept only feet away.

Feeling the breeze from the open terrace doors, Missy decided some fresh air might be just what she needed. Stepping outside, she drew in a deep breath. The evening air was warm and the dress she wore made it seem even warmer. Ronald never allowed her to wear anything other than the long dresses that covered everything. He never allowed her to show any flesh. She waved that thought away and rubbed the cut on her arm. It was itchy, the heat making her sweat; the sweat stung the open wound. She needed to give her wounds air and cool down.

Stepping inside, leaving the patio doors slightly ajar, she wandered to her bedroom and began to undress. A shower would help. She caught her reflection in the mirror and examined the cut on her neck. It was healing, slowly, but still oozed in places. It needed air. Unfortunately, leaving her collar open wasn't an option. That would stir too many questions. Turning on the cool water, she stepped under the stream and let the water wash the sweat away.

Why was it people felt the need to pry into someone else's life? Couldn't they just be satisfied with what they saw? She just wasn't comfortable being picked apart and would rather no one knew of her life before coming here, or what she had run from. Missy preferred to leave that in the past.

Joanne Morrow died two days ago, on the floor with a knife at her neck, and Missy Green had been born. She wouldn't mourn a woman who had been dominated, controlled, abused. She would move on, and be a better person, *be* Missy Green.

What sort of past did Missy have? None. Therefore, when asked about her life, asked who Missy really was, she hadn't lied. As of two days ago, Missy Green hadn't existed. There wasn't much to tell when someone had only been born days ago.

Missy was single, she decided. Had never been engaged, especially not to a cold-hearted bastard like Ronald O'Connor. Missy had no life. Not yet at least. She had to build one first. Maybe it was a good thing that she'd come here and stayed. It would give her time to figure out what to do with her life. It would give her time to regain her strength, to compose herself, to become whole again. Amazing, she thought, in the days since she'd run from Ronald, she felt as if she could finally breathe again. Taking in a deep breath, she smiled, maybe for the first time in years, and it felt good.

There was no fear, no tension, and no stress. It was her prerogative to sing in the shower, however off-key it might be. If she chose to wear pants and a tank top, she was free to do so. She could lie in bed for hours and read and no one could tell her to get up and stop being lazy. She no longer had to deal with insults about her singing, her clothing, or her lack of expertise in the bedroom And no one, absolutely no one, would ever control her, beat her, or make her feel small. She was a free woman now, truly free.

Lifting her arms in the air, water spilling over her body, she laughed. She was free and nothing or nobody would ever prevent her from that freedom. From this day on, there was no past, only a future. No yesterdays, only tomorrows. For the first time in her life, she went to bed completely naked, alone and loving it. Closing her eyes, she felt safe and secure.

But in her dreams, her past wouldn't co-operate. She was tormented, tortured, and abused repeatedly while she slept, and it left her feeling as helpless as she had at the hands of her fiancé.

Chapter Four

Draco mingled, smiling with the charm that came so naturally to him, and watched the crowd as they conversed amongst themselves. They chatted about their lives and mutual interest in the stars. Some were quite knowledgeable. Yet Missy stayed to the back, quiet, alone. Oh, she smiled when approached, chatted when spoken to, but always, he sensed, she held back. When the conversation came to be about her and her life, she diverted the questions, leaving the person none the wiser.

Draco was certain she was hiding something. It just added to his already budding interest in the raven-haired beauty with mesmerizing eyes. He needed to know who she was, now.

Leaving his guests in capable hands, he went to his office, calling to Hunter with his mind.

"What have you got for me?" Draco asked the instant Hunter entered the room.

Hunter drew in a labored breath. "I'm afraid to say I have nothing, sir."

"Nothing?" Draco shifted his dark, stern eyes to Hunter.

"Yes sir, there is no Missy Green on my list."

"How is that possible?"

"I don't know, sir. I've gone over the list several times and her name is not there. We didn't send out an invitation to a Missy Green."

"Explain to me how she managed to get on the bus?"

"I don't know, sir. I did a head count and there are thirty-one people when there should only be thirty."

"She got on the bus without a ticket, without anyone noticing her? Imbeciles." He'd planned it perfectly, selecting thirty people at a time, twenty being women of a certain age. Now, he had someone who wasn't on the list, whom he knew nothing about. That pissed him off. "Find out who she is, Hunter."

"Yes, sir."

Draco rubbed his chin and looked out his patio doors. "Have her meet me in my suite for dinner." He would get to the bottom of this, carefully. Find out who she really was. However, he didn't want to spook her, so he would have to be smooth in doing so.

"Yes, sir." Hunter tipped his head of thinning grey hair before hurrying from the room.

Closing his eyes, rubbing his temples, Draco wished just once his people would do their jobs without screwing it up.

She had no idea why she'd be invited to a private dinner with her host, but once again her politeness surged up and she accepted.

Standing at his door, Missy wanted nothing more than to bolt. There was barely time for that thought when the door opened and Draco stood smiling at her from the other side.

"Come in." He took her hand to his lips and they both jolted at the quick zap. "I must tell Hunter to turn the humidity up in the house. I am so glad you could join me, Missy."

He was a charmer. "I'm honored to be invited," she

murmured.

He released her hand and she stepped inside his suite. It was the size of an average condominium and decorated very lavishly.

He chose smooth tones here, creams and browns. Odd, she thought. She'd pictured his suite in darker colors, considering that's what he'd worn, all the times she'd seen him before. Looking at his smooth jacket and pants, she saw he hadn't disappointed her. Once again he wore black, including the shirt. This time, however, there was no tie and the first few buttons of his shirt were open. It made him look rather...well, sexy.

"The honor is all mine." He led her to a small table draped in white lace, a burning candle in the center, and held the chair for her. "It's not often that I get to dine with a stunningly beautiful young lady such as yourself." He smiled at her with a flirtatious warmth that didn't escape her.

"That's very kind of you." She watched him as he walked around the small table and took a seat directly across from her. He was smooth, very smooth, and emitted elegance and charm.

"It was meant with honesty. Are you settling in all right?" Lifting the bottle of wine that sat in the bucket of ice on a tray beside the table, he poured her glass first, then his, before he set the wine bottle away.

"Yes, thank you. My room is lovely." She thought to tell him she didn't drink but decided it would be rude and let it go.

"Glad you like it. The telephones are at your disposal, should you need to make a call."

"Thank you. I'll keep that in mind." She smiled politely.

"That's a lovely dress. The soft blue is a beautiful contrast against your dark hair."

She was uncomfortable with his compliment. "Thank you."

"And the silk scarf is a nice accent, though I think it would look better in your hair."

If he knew why she wore it..."I'll keep that in mind."

She flinched when the doors to his suite opened, and took a

breath when she saw it was Hunter. He carried a tray with plates that gave off the most tantalizing aroma. They had her mouth watering.

"I hope you like what I had made for us?"

Missy smiled up at Hunter as he set her plate before her. She drew in the scent of rice and chicken, a distinct aroma of almonds, not overpowering but tantalizing. "It smells wonderful."

"Thank you, Hunter." Draco waited for him to leave before continuing. "I have to confess something. I find you simply fascinating, Missy."

She wished now she'd been rude and declined. "I'm just an ordinary person."

"You are too modest. When were you born?"

His question caught her off guard. Her first thought was to lie; however, she saw no real harm in telling him. "September tenth, nineteen seventy-eight." She forked up a piece of chicken, deciding to turn the tables. "How about you?" she asked, calmly sliding the fork into her mouth.

His eyes brightened with interest as an amused grin filled his face. "Oh, when you get to be my age, birthdays are irrelevant."

"You don't look that old to me." She took another small bite and studied him a little more closely. He wasn't old, not ancient at least, probably younger than her father. Maybe forty, at best.

As he lifted his wine, a grin filled his face and showed a sweeter side of Draco. "You flatter me, but I assure you, looks can be deceiving."

She knew that all too well. "True, but with your looks, you don't have much to worry about with age. Men always look better as they grow older." She ate slowly, wiping her mouth after every bite.

"You'll make me blush with talk like that."

Her eyes fell to her plate. She hadn't meant to flirt. "How long have you lived here?" She changed the subject while she kept her eyes on her food.

"Oh, it seems like forever."

He was definitely being evasive. "I've never been to Erie before."

"Oh? It's not far from Middletown. I assume that's where you lived, given that was the stop on the tour."

"Yes, that was my home."

"Is that where you were born as well?

He was awfully nosy. "No, I was born in Philadelphia. Do you have family?" She ate while questioning him, turning it back to him.

"No, unfortunately, I'm all alone."

Was that a bit of sadness she heard in his voice? "Never married?" Her plate was nearly empty and she found she was rather enjoying herself. Who would have thought? She noticed he had barely touched his food, though, which was odd.

"No, not so far. It seems I've waited too long for the right woman to be my wife and bear me children."

Definitely sadness there. "It's never too late."

"Perhaps, perhaps not." He swirled his wine.

She lifted her glass of water and sipped. "You could always adopt." Was that why he invited people to his home to learn about the stars? Was he lonely and sought out company?

He forked up a small amount of chicken. "It's not quite the same as having one of your own."

She sighed as she rested her fork on her plate. "There are so many children out there waiting for someone to claim them and give them a home. More people should adopt."

"Those words have a great deal of sentiment. Were you one of those many children, Missy? Were you adopted?"

She paused, shifted the tiny bits of rice left on her plate. What would it hurt if she spoke the truth? "Yes, I was." She had been raised by the most caring and loving people imaginable. She felt melancholy, missing her family, regretting not being able to call them, to lean on them. But it was best they didn't get involved right now.

"How old were you when you were adopted?"

"Only a few days old. I was lucky. Not all children are taken into a loving home."

"You were raised well?"

She cleared her throat, shifted in her chair. She hadn't meant to get into her life. "Yes."

"You are one of the lucky ones. Perhaps you would like to call your family, and let them know how you are doing."

She sipped her water and thought of her father. Was he worried about her? "That's fine; they won't be worried about me." It hurt so much to tell that lie. She knew in her heart that her father would be worried. They all would be.

"Have you been away from home long?" Lifting his wine, he watched her over the rim.

"Long enough." She stood, to hell with politeness. She needed to go before too much was let out. She couldn't afford to give too much of herself. "Thank you for inviting me to dinner. It was lovely."

He stood as she did, surprise on his face. "Leaving so soon? We haven't had desert."

"Yes, I'm afraid so. I'm rather tired."

"Your name isn't on my list."

She froze midway from rising out of her chair. "Excuse me?"

"I sent out invitations to a select number of people to participate in my Starr Gazers excursion. Your name is not on that list."

"I'm sorry. I...uh...overheard some people talking about where they were going and I thought it might be fascinating to learn more about the stars. I can leave—"

"No need to rush off. Far be it for me to stand in the way of such an eager mind." His smile turned an already handsome face devastatingly gorgeous. "You're welcome to stay as long as you like."

What a kind gesture, she thought. "Thank you. I...uh...should go. I think the trip is catching up with me. I'm rather tired." Turning, she headed for the door. She nearly jumped, her breath caught, as he appeared before her. She hadn't even seen him move, or heard him for that fact. The man was fast.

"I wouldn't want to overtire you. Thank you for joining me for dinner, Missy." He held the door, his smile soft. "Pleasant dreams."

"Thank you." With that said, she hurried away.

Reluctant to let her go, Draco watched as she hurried off before he closed the door. "Your departure was too hurried, Missy Green. Did I touch a nerve?" Turning away from the door, he snapped his fingers and Hunter appeared.

"Yes, sir."

"She was adopted." A flick of his wrist and Draco held a lit cigarette between his long, elegant fingers. "And she was born at the time of the halfling. I want all the birth records pulled from September tenth to the fifteenth, nineteen seventy-eight."

"Interesting, sir. Did she indicate where she was born?"

"Yes. Philadelphia."

"I'll get right on it."

"Perfect!" He snapped his fingers and Hunter disappeared into thin air.

Could it be? Could she be the one?

His patience was running thin. He had to find out who she was, and now. Something about her possessed him, transfixing him, not just with her beauty or those damned warm-yet-sad pools of gold, but something else. He knew it was taboo to be with her, but something about her called to him. He'd never felt such a strong urge before now. It was as if she were pulling at him, drawing him to her. The sooner he knew all there was to know about her, the sooner he might be able to figure out what it was that drew him in so deeply. He rested a hip on the corner of his desk and took a drag of his cigarette.

He was tired of being lonely. He'd lived centuries, had been happy living out his days causing havoc, running amuck in a world oblivious to his kind, collecting souls for Satan. Then the loneliness had set in. At first, he'd thought he had been freed of Satan's control and allowed to start his own life. Though no longer called to take lives, it had been a thrill for him, and possibly, that was what he missed. He'd freelanced, in a way, taking lives when he had the urge. Yet still his heart felt heavy, his days tedious. Not even his wealth and business fulfilled him. With each passing year, he found himself feeling even more at odds.

Very few people knew that he was a demon, let alone one feared by many. Oh, people still feared him, his employees mostly, and that was enough for him, now. It hadn't always been that way, though. He hadn't always had this feeling of incredible emptiness. When he'd heard, through the grapevine, so to speak, that a child had been born to a demon and a human, Draco had begun his search for the Halfling on that day.

Drawing one last time on his cigarette, Draco used his powers to wave it away. He sat alone in his office, longing for a woman he knew he could never have, and feeling the weight of that need rip through him.

Chapter Five

In the days that followed the meal with Draco and the revelation that he knew she'd sneaked onto his bus, Missy was glad she managed to see very little of him. It was kind of him to allow her to stay in his home. Still, she felt a little awkward around him.

She kept to herself, mostly, when Jennifer would allow it. Attending the nightly stargazing lessons, Missy listened while the instructors discussed the constellations. It was fascinating, more so than she'd thought possible. She found it odd that their host never attended any of the nightly rituals. One would think he would head the classes. Then again, the guy was a little odd, in her opinion. What sort of person invited strangers into his home, giving them lessons on stargazing with the promise of a job? There was something not right about the whole deal, yet she found herself sticking around nonetheless. He did have his moments, like when he'd encouraged her to call her family.

She missed them terribly.

Missy wondered if her father or her siblings had learned she'd left Ronald yet. Surely, he must have called looking for her, and she knew they would worry. She'd thought to call her family, since Draco gave her permission to use the phones, but she hadn't, wouldn't, couldn't. Not yet.

Maybe in a few days she would call them to reassure them she was all right. She just wasn't ready to explain to them why she'd left, or all she'd endured. There was too much shame inside of her to talk about it just yet.

Sitting in her room, missing the ones she loved, Missy wished she could just make everything that she'd endured simply vanish. Go back in time to when Ronald first approached her, and refused his interest in her. If only she'd known then what she knew now.

Sighing, she leaned back and a tiny tear slid from her eye. It wasn't as if she could turn back time. No one could. What was done was done.

Time to move on.

Wiping her face clean, Missy decided she'd wallowed long enough. Unlike everyone else, she didn't want to lounge under the baking-hot sun or chat with friends. She was too restless for that. Being catered to, having her room cleaned, weren't things she was used to. She'd always been inundated with chores, which included making sure the house was spotless from top to bottom before Ronald returned from work.

Missy shook her head to bring herself back to the present. She decided to explore her surroundings, and left the security of her room.

"Good afternoon, Missy. I thought everyone was out enjoying the sunshine."

She jumped at Draco's voice behind her. It always seemed like he appeared out of nowhere. "They are. But I've never been much for lying around in the sun," she admitted freely.

"It seems we have that in common. I, too, prefer to be kept busy."

She doubted there were many common factors between her and the debonair Mr. Starr. "I was just looking for something to do to occupy my time."

His eyes grew even darker when he was intrigued. "Did you have something in mind?"

She shrugged, glancing around. "I don't suppose you need

help cleaning this enormous mansion?"

"You'd like to clean my home?"

Now she felt awkward. "Well...it's just...I feel like I should contribute in some way, to pay you back for your generosity."

"There's no need to repay me. But I can see when a person needs something to do and I am happy to help you out." He smiled charmingly. Taking hold of her elbow, Draco led her along. "I think I might have the perfect job to keep you busy. I do believe my library is in need of dusting." He flung large oak doors open to a room filled with shelves of books. "Do you think this would keep you busy?"

Her mouth nearly fell open. A laugh escaped in place of it. "For some time." There had to be thousands of books in there.

"You should laugh more often. The sound is...musical, and your face lights up."

It suddenly occurred to her just how close he'd gotten to her. Wanting distance, she moved to one of the shelves. "This is quite a collection."

"I like to read. Do you like to read, Missy?"

He was making her so uncomfortable. "If the right book comes my way. I'll need some supplies."

"Of course. I'll send my housekeeper for them. Do I make you uncomfortable, Missy?"

A nervous giggle slipped out. "Of course not."

"Are you sure?" he took a step closer to her and she backed away. "I mean you no harm."

"I would like to get started on the shelves now." His presence, his closeness, made her heart speed up but oddly, not from fear. It had been so long since she'd felt an attraction to a man that she didn't know what to do about it.

"Of course. I'll go see about those supplies for you now."

The instant he left, she let out a huge breath.

Draco entered his office after instructing the housekeeper

to provide Missy with the necessary cleaning supplies. The looks he'd received had been rather amusing. He knew perfectly well his housekeepers were territorial about cleaning, but he reassured them everything would go back to the norm once Missy was able to relieve some of her restlessness.

"Hunter," he summoned.

"Yes, sir." Hunter appeared in the room.

"What have you got for me?"

"I have the information, sir, and you are not going to believe this." Hunter handed Draco the file. "I asked the maid for the room key to search Missy's belongings for identification. Missy Green is not who she says she is."

"Oh?" His curiosity was piqued.

"Her real name is Joanne Morrow and I suspect she snuck onto the bus...well, I'll let you read the file and come to your own conclusion." Hunter beamed.

"Interesting. Thank you, Hunter."

With a bow of his head, Hunter left the room.

Using the power of his mind, Draco slid a chair from across the room toward him. It came to a stop neatly behind him. He lowered himself to the chair, and laid the file on his lap.

Draco sat in calm silence while he read the contents of the file.

Baby girl Dawson, born September tenth, nineteen seventy-eight. Mother: Michelle Dawson, deceased. Father: Unknown. Infant adopted four days after birth by Dr. Richard Morrow and wife Janet Morrow. Three natural children: Bradley Richard, Connor Ray, and Patricia Leah.

All three children were older than Missy. Why adopt after having three natural children of your own, he wondered. With a wave of his hand, the page flipped over.

An engagement announcement was next. Interesting, he thought.

It is with delight that Dr. Richard and Janet Morrow announce the engagement of our daughter, Joanne Marie Morrow, to Ronald Dean O'Connor of Middletown.

Engaged. Interesting that you should omit that piece of information, Missy, or should I say, Joanne, he thought. So Missy Green is really Joanne Morrow. He conjured up a cigarette, and contemplated the name. He preferred Missy. It suited to her more though he wondered how she'd come to have it.

"It appears you've fled your fiancé. Now why would that be, Missy?" Drawing on his cigarette, he studied the file before him. "Secrets never stay buried for long." Leaning back in his chair, he waved his hand and the file floated effortlessly to his desk, landing perfectly on top.

"After tonight's ceremonies are finished, I might just have to confront you." He smiled slyly. Toying with his cigarette, he wrapped his fingers around it and crushed it out in his bare hand. When he opened his hand, the cigarette was gone, leaving behind nothing but its scent.

It had been hours since Missy dug into the task of cleaning the many shelves in the library. She was exhausted, but felt great. It was just what she needed to rid herself of all the pent-up energy she'd been feeling.

Hunter had brought dinner to her when she hadn't gone to join the others, and she was grateful for it. The solitude was a welcome change. By ten that evening she'd cleaned every shelf and felt satisfied that she'd done a superb job. Draco had an interesting array of books, some that left her wondering about the owner. There were books of almost every kind, ranging from romance to suspense, horror and westerns, self-help books as well as poetry. There had been the darker novels, some with names that were impossible to pronounce and others that were written in some sort of language she couldn't discern. She assessed that his tastes were rather eclectic.

It would be a nice change to curl up with one of the many books from the shelves.

Rolling her aching shoulders, Missy left the library in search of a housekeeper to hand over her supplies. The house seemed to be virtually empty and she figured the staff had long since gone to bed. She left the cleaning supplies in the kitchen, which gave her more than a moment of envy. She'd never seen such a huge kitchen, or one as pristine.

She decided to go to Draco and thank him for giving her something to do. He'd surprised her by his gesture and the least she could do was show her appreciation. She knocked once on his office door, then waited, before knocking once more. Receiving no answer, she decided to leave him a note instead. Inching the door open, she hoped he didn't mind her intruding on his space. She'd only be a moment, in any case.

Crossing the room to his desk, she searched for a slip of paper to leave her note. She could always wait to thank him in person, but...well, their earlier encounter still made her feel uneasy. She pushed a file folder aside and found a small pad. Preparing to write the note, she stopped abruptly when she heard voices approaching the room. Terrified at being caught in his office, Missy ran to the back of the room, to what she thought was another exit. What it was instead was a tiny closet. She ducked inside, her heart racing. The sounds drew closer and she recognized both Draco and Jennifer's voices. Inching the door open, she watched them both enter the room.

"I feel so honored that you would want to share a drink with me in private." Jennifer gushed.

"The honor is truly mine."

Missy saw him walk to the liquor cabinet only feet from where she hid. He pulled out two glasses, and began to pour a healthy dose of something red from a beautiful crystal decanter. He reached into his jacket pocket and pulled out a tiny glass vial. She watched as he dropped some of the yellow liquid into one of the glasses. What was he doing?

"It is so enjoyable to be in the company of a beauty such as yourself." He carried the glasses, handing one to Jennifer as he met her in the seating area.

Jennifer took down most of the glass in one gulp. "Wow, that packs a hell of a punch. Quite the place you have here. Big," she laughed and gulped down more of the liquid.

"I like my space."

"Looks like. And that yard. I would hate to take care of that." She laughed again, drank some more. "I can't tell you how excited I am to be here, Mr. Starr."

"Please, call me Draco."

"Draco it is." She wavered, stumbling. "Man, that's powerful stuff." The glass in her hand fell to the floor with a hard clunk, bouncing on the rug before coming to a stop on its side, several inches away. Jennifer swayed and as her knees gave out, Draco caught her in his arms.

"Now, let's see if you're the one."

Her body frozen in fear, Missy watched with curious interest at what was transpiring. He laid Jennifer on the sofa, took off his suit jacket, and rolled up his sleeves. Missy fixed her eyes on Draco. She watched and listened as he spoke in a language she couldn't understand. It almost sounded like gibberish.

Suddenly, right before her eyes, she saw him transform. It was like some weird nightmare that she was unable to wake up from. He seemed to be turning into...a monster. His body changed, expanded. His face took on a look of ribbed leather and the hands he held up in the air became longer, his fingernails extending. As he opened his mouth, she saw several sharp, pointed teeth, much like those of a wolf.

What the hell was he?

Locked in place, fear holding her, she was helpless to do anything but watch.

"*In is terra EGO peto thee. Parvulus of Diabolus, Parvulus of Deus. Exorior exhibeo vestri volo,*" Draco called out, his arms held over Jennifer. His head tipped back. His eyes closed.

A wave of dizziness took hold and Missy slid to the floor. She heard Jennifer cry out and as she lifted her head and peered out through the crack, she saw Jennifer run for the door.

"Please, stay calm." Draco caught her by the arms, held her in place.

Jennifer threw her arms up, slipped out from his control and began running about the room like a madwoman. She tossed furniture, smashed lamps, slammed her body into the walls.

"Stop!"

Through blurry eyes, a fog numbing her brain, Missy watched in stunned bewilderment. What she saw couldn't be real. Draco began to chant louder, again in a language that made no sense to her. Choking on a gasp, she watched as Jennifer began to tear at her own flesh.

"Sweet Lucifer!" He ran to Jennifer, and grabbing hold of her head in his hands, twisted it.

Missy heard a loud snap as Jennifer's head wrenched sharply to the side, and watched as Jennifer fell like a rag doll to the floor. Draco chanted something and in a flash, both were gone.

Missy stumbled from the closet, gasping for the air that seemed to refuse her lungs. Placing a hand to her chest, she could have sworn her heart no longer beat. In tiny spurts, the air came back, leaving her feeling dizzy and disoriented. But she knew enough to get out. Clawing her way across the room, standing on wobbly legs, Missy grabbed hold of the door, and pulled it open.

She had to get away.

Chapter Six

Stumbling up the stairs, Missy managed to make it to her suite. Her chest was on fire, her vision blurry. She staggered into her room, bumping into furniture in her way. The vision of what she'd just witnessed spiked like hot daggers in her mind. He killed her. Had he become something worse than a monster and killed Jennifer? Or am I delirious?

A sudden piercing pain sent Missy crashing to the floor, clutching her body. Her vision turned an odd shade of red; the room spun all around her. Without warning, she found herself convulsing. Her arms flailed, her legs kicked out, as she bounced on the floor. It felt as if something were trying to break free from inside her. Her eyes flew open as the stabbing sliced deep into her gut. She curled into a ball, sobbing, as pain exploded inside her.

It seemed to last forever, the pain in her belly, stabbing her chest, her bones aching with an intensity she'd never felt before. The rush of noise erupting in her head made her cry out, and she reached up with her hands to clasp hold of her skull. It was so loud, like a train roaring inside her mind. Her muscles twitching, her legs, arms, torso, convulsing uncontrollably, as she tried to comprehend what was happening.

Everything hurt. She could feel the carpet beneath her as if it were made of steel wool instead of fine silken fibers. The air around her seemed to lash out at her skin, whipping against what felt like raw flesh, with nasty slashes. She opened her eyes and was struck blind.

"Help," she cried out, but her voice seemed so distant.

Managing to get to her knees, Missy tried to crawl her way to where she thought the door was. Her nails caught on the rug, and as she tugged them free, she felt one snap. She bumped into furniture, blindly trying to get help. The nausea struck her suddenly.

She needed the washroom, now!

The cold linoleum floor beneath her hands shocked her, and as she moved about, she bumped into the toilet. Baffled as to how she'd gotten there, Missy lifted up and hung her head over the toilet. What came from inside tasted dreadful, like rancid meat, and burned like acid.

· Exhausted, she collapsed on the floor, suddenly feeling hollow, empty inside. Closing her eyes, she drew in a few deep breaths, and it felt as if she were underwater. She coughed, and her lungs stung as if they had been torn open. The cold hit her unexpectedly, as if she'd stepped into a freezing winter storm, chilling her right to the bone. Opening her eyes, she could finally see—though everything looked fuzzy—she crawled her way to her bed. Pulling herself up, she curled into the blankets, wrapping them around her as she shivered, her teeth chattering.

There voices inside her head were so loud they were deafening. Clasping her hands over her ears, she rocked her body, wishing the voices away.

"*What time is it?*"

"*Come on baby, just a quick hand job.*"

"*I don't wanna sleep.*"

"*I want my mommy.*"

"*In the news tonight...*"

"*Freeze!*"

"You cheated on me, you bastard!"

"Stop it! Stop it! Stop it!" Missy cried out, begging for the voices to leave her alone. Her body ached from the cold that filled her from inside out. She was absolutely unable to get warm. Pushing from the bed, she stumbled back to the washroom. She turned the hot-water faucet on full blast before stripping out of her clothing. Stepping beneath the steaming spray, she yelped when the water scalded her and quickly turned on the cold tap. She slid to the tub floor, letting the warm water run over her chilled body.

What was happening to her?

The air around her wavered before everything went black.

Draco paced his room with wide angry steps, a cloud of grey smoke trailing behind him from the cigarette he puffed. He heard Hunter enter the room but didn't bother with hospitality. "She was not the one and—" He spun around to face Hunter. "I had to kill her!"

"Are you all right, sir?"

"No!" He waved the cigarette away and willed himself a glass of blood wine. "She became hysterical. I don't know what came over her. She actually began clawing at her own flesh. I've never seen a reaction like that. There was nothing else I could do."

"How horrible."

"Indeed. Her mind snapped. I could feel it, the moment she woke and saw me. She must have been mentally unstable."

"I'm sorry, sir."

Draco gulped down his wine, waved the glass away. "How many females are left?"

"Six."

"I don't understand why she became so frantic." He paced the floor in sharp, anxious steps. "She seemed very normal when I invited her to my office...but the drug took hold quite quickly. It baffles me why it didn't last as long as all the other times."

"Perhaps we didn't calculate her weight properly. She might have given me the wrong number during my interrogations."

"That must be it." Had to be it. "I can't see anyone tonight. I need to stay away from the humans until I feel more myself." He was much too frustrated and angry to be around humans right now. "Damn it! I'm tired of waiting."

"I know, sir. I know. If you need anything—"

"I have but to call. I know. Thank you, Hunter." As Hunter vanished, Draco lit another cigarette. He felt restless. Stepping out onto his terrace, he looked up at the night sky and drew in the warm air.

He'd lived for centuries, done some horrible things in his time on earth, but since starting Starr Industries, he'd tried to live clean. It wasn't good business to feed off of the very people he worked alongside. He'd done his time as soul stealer for Satan, and now, it was his turn to live as he chose.

He wondered what Satan would do if he knew the halfling was still alive and not dead, as her father Pythos had proclaimed. He'd been so cocky, standing up to their master, insisting he'd known nothing of the human he'd impregnated. Being one of Satan's cherished minions gave Pythos a great sense of security. It was his mistake to think Satan would forgive him. But Satan knew, he always knew. Lucifer was not so kind. And Draco was sure he'd be just as merciless to the child Pythos had conceived.

Draco was sure Lucifer would want her dead, given his lack of control over her human side. Well, he sure as hell wasn't going to let Lucifer know he was searching for her, or that she was indeed alive.

Drawing heavily on his cigarette, Draco sent it away as he stared out into the darkness. He had everything he could possibly want. Money, prestige, respect, but the one thing he longed for more than anything was a companion. He'd so hoped to have found her this evening. Another disappointment.

He'd begun searching for the Halfling three years earlier, when he'd first learned that the child had survived. Neither Satan or Pythos had divulged that to him.

Yet after three years, he was still no closer to finding her than when he'd started. And having to drink from one of the humans tonight had not been in his plan.

She had to be out there somewhere.

In the beginning, Draco tried scoping out the bars in search of her. But after months of enduring loud music of various genres and fighting his way through the crowds, he'd grown tired of it. Traveling the world had been the only high point to the search. So he'd founded the Starr Gazers and with his employees' help, searched the world over for females born at the time of the halfling's birth. He'd sent out thousands of invitations, hoping one would be the halfling. What young person could refuse a free all-expenses paid vacation with the promise of employment? So far the response had been good, but still no halfling.

Where was she, and why couldn't he find her?

He needed air, needed freedom. With only a thought, he sent himself soaring over cities, over towns, over villages, wondering if she was hidden somewhere below. He needed to release his tension, the frustration of disappointment, the urge to drink. High above the cities and towns, Draco soared, incognito. He watched as people milled about, as people went on with their meaningless, tired lives. He'd never wanted that life, was grateful he had so much more. His existence wasn't meaningless. He worked. By day he was a businessman. By night, his demon persona came free, but only in the privacy of his rooms.

But there were times, like now, that he needed to let loose, needed to be...himself. Oh, he'd given up terrorizing people long ago, but at times like this, he missed it. Hovering high in the darkened night, he wondered what would happen if he flew down and caused a minor disaster.

He knew what would happen. He would be discovered, or rather, what he was would be discovered. It would be in all the papers, on the news, and speculation would arise. He didn't need that, preferred living normally, well, as normally as a demon could in a world of skeptics and a populace hostile to the abnormal.

No, Draco Starr, once the most fearsome of all monsters, would not give in, would not slip back to what he had been. He was on a mission, and that mission was love. Soaring up high, higher, he dallied amongst the stars that lay ruse to his search.

In her dreams, Missy was chased by a monster with jagged teeth and clawed fingers. He ran after her, growling like a madman, calling out to her. And when he caught up to her, pinning her to the ground, his face changed and he became her fiancé.

She woke to a violent fit of vomiting. Barely making it to the washroom, she spilled the contents of her stomach so hard it made her head throb and her body ache. When it was finally over, she got to her feet and walked to the sink to splash cold water on her face. Glancing up and into the mirror, she let out a gasp at what she saw. Her eyes were red, her face was ribbed and her mouth...dear God, she looked like Draco when he'd attacked Jennifer.

She blinked, and the vision was gone.

She was hallucinating. She must be. What other reason was there for what she'd just seen? Her legs could barely carry her, yet she managed to make it to the bed. It felt as if she'd been run over by a steamroller. She was acutely aware of every pore in her skin, every nerve ending, every muscle in her body. She could even feel the blood as it rushed through her veins. It was almost as though her body were reforming, from each tiny cell, to the greater being. Her bones ached, her skin burned, much like when she'd been a teen experiencing growing pains, only ten times worse. She curled up on the bed in a fetal position, and waited out the pain.

How was it possible to feel each breath expand her lungs, then deflate as the air was expelled? Yet she felt it, saw it. It wasn't possible to see her heart pumping, ever so slowly, while blood rushed through each artery to fill her veins. How was it possible she could see every internal organ as if it were on a TV screen before her?

Her mind was fuzzy and reeling with everything that was happening to her.

How had she gotten here? Where was here? Lifting her head, she glanced around the tidy room and recognition hit.

Dear God, what had she seen?

Flashes, like clips from a movie, played in her mind. Jennifer laughing, Draco serving drinks, Jennifer passing out. Draco transforming into a monster, Jennifer clawing violently at her own flesh. Draco and Jennifer, simply vanishing.

He'd gone from a dark handsome man to a hideous creature in seconds flat. That wasn't possible: she must have been hallucinating. There was no such thing as vampires, demons, or monsters. Yet, what she saw in that room defied all logic.

Her stomach rolled over, once, twice before it sent her scrambling back to the washroom. It seemed like hours she hung over the cool porcelain, spewing nothing at all yet something so vile, it tasted like acid. When her body was finally spent, she leaned against the cold tub and tried to draw in enough air to prevent herself from blacking out.

What was wrong with her? Why did she feel so dreadfully ill? Her vision blurred, her head swam. She wished she was back in her bed. The floor beneath her disappeared and she floated up until she lay once more on the soft mattress.

She cradled her body, arms around legs, legs pulled to her chest. She was so cold, so deathly cold. The chills caused her teeth to chatter so loudly, sounding like drums pounding fiercely, it startled her. No amount of blankets could help; a fire brewing beside her wouldn't have been able to keep her warm.

The chills subsided and the heat took over, scorching heat, so hot she felt as if she were burning up. She couldn't escape; it seemed to come from inside, deep inside. Her body thrashed about in bed. She tried to fight the fire burning her from within. She drifted in and out, fading from consciousness to unconscious, over and over again. She had no idea how long she fought but was grateful when she was finally granted a reprieve. Her body leveled, the heat cooled, the ache subsided, and her body became painless, effortless, and calm.

Closing her eyes, she drifted off.

CHAPTER SEVEN

The morning came as it always did, bright and cheery, only Missy wasn't aware of it. The sleep that captured her during the night held her deep in its womb. Nightmares plagued her, fought with her, and she struggled to break free. Beasts reared their ugly heads, stole victims from their beds, and devoured the life that once breathed air.

Suddenly, she was the beast, curbing a hunger she never thought possible. Running free, in the darkness, she sought out victims to fill her needs. Bodies, endless bodies, lay in her wake. The hunger was so great she found herself tearing through flesh with jagged teeth. She tasted the blood, the flesh, and craved more.

The revelation had her bolting up, her eyes wide. She wasn't a savage beast; she hadn't fed off of humans. Yet, she tasted the nightmare still in her mouth.

Her head ached, her body throbbed. The sunlight faded, she drifted in and out, visions so clear she thought she was living them. Surfacing some time later to utter darkness, Missy glanced at the clock and frowned at the time. She could have sworn it had just been daylight, the sun piercing her eyes, stabbing into her head. Yet, now, it was dark.

Was it possible she'd slept the day away? Pushing the covers aside, she was shocked to see her body completely nude. She had no recollection of undressing, let alone crawling into bed for that fact. With wobbly legs, she climbed from the bed to grab her robe. Why was she so weak?

She'd been ill, terribly ill; her aching body reminded her of that. The taste in her mouth repulsed her. What she needed was a hot shower and food to fill her empty stomach.

She frowned at the knock on the door. She was in no mood or condition for company. She chose to ignore it. When the knocking became more persistent, she gave in and went to it. Belting her robe, she opened the door and her blood ran cold.

"Good evening, Missy. I do hope I haven't disturbed you?"

Missy's hand lay frozen on the door. It hadn't been a dream, she had seen it. Behind this handsome face lay a hideous monster with sharp, jagged teeth. Where was that monster now?

"You're pale. Are you ill?" He reached a hand out to her and she jumped back.

"I'm fine. Just the flu, I think." The room swayed, a grey fog lifted over her vision, and she teetered.

He grabbed her before she fell and helped her to the sofa. "You need a doctor. I'll order my physician to assist you. I'll go ring for him."

"No, I'm fine. Really," she proclaimed as he hurried to the phone. She didn't want anything from him but for him to leave her alone.

"You are not fine. You nearly blacked out at the door. Dr. Thornton, I need you in suite four immediately." He hung up the phone and hurried back to the sofa. "The doctor will be here momentarily."

"You have a doctor on call?"

"Yes. Can I get you anything?"

She shifted further away from him, shaking her head. "I just need to rest."

"And you will, just as soon as the doctor examines you." He

bolted up the instant the knock sounded on the door. "Thank you for hurrying, Doctor. Right this way. Her name is Missy and she nearly blacked out on me when she answered the door."

"I'll check her out. Give me a few moments."

"Of course."

The instant Draco was gone, Missy let out a long breath. "I'm really fine, Doctor. There's no need for you to examine me." She really didn't want him near her. All she wanted was to go back to sleep and forget what she'd seen.

"If Draco is concerned for your health, it is best I look after you. I won't be a minute."

Giving in, she answered the doctor's questions, explaining that she felt sick to her stomach and dizzy. He listened to her heartbeat, felt her pulse, and in the end told her to rest and drink plenty of fluids.

It was exactly what she'd planned in any case.

He helped her to her bedroom, making sure she was safely tucked in before he left the room. He seemed like a nice, elderly man and she wondered if he lived here in the house. How else would he have been here so quickly?

Pulling the blankets up, she closed her eyes she fell asleep.

Pacing the floor, Draco smoked like a madman. He'd never felt worry for a human before. It was a feeling he was far from comfortable with and was clueless on how to deal with it. There was just something about Missy that drew him in.

Beauty, she had been graced with an abundance. Spirit, he felt there must be a wealth of it hidden beneath the shy exterior. There was fear and caution in her eyes, and what eyes they were. He'd never seen eyes of gold before, so pure without a single flaw. And they always seemed to call to him.

This young woman had come into his home by accident and mesmerized him upon first glance. He'd never felt anything like it before and had no explanation as to why he was so taken with her. He'd had women before, his fair share over the centuries, but never had one drawn him in so completely that he found it hard to think of anything else.

It was silly of him to think of her in any case. He needed to find a mate. Yet, he was transfixed by this raven-haired beauty with golden eyes. What the hell was he supposed to do now? She was human; he was not. How could he want something so deeply that was not his for the taking, that was forbidden to him? Yet, he did. He wanted her, not just once, nor twice, but more, so much more.

"I've left her to sleep," Dr. Thornton explained as he entered the room.

Draco turned, his eyes filled with worry. "Will she be all right?" Where was all this anxiety coming from?

"She'll be fine, with plenty of rest and lots of liquids. Maybe a little run down, definitely underweight."

"Thank you, Doctor." Draco tipped his head before hurrying from the room. The need to see Missy was overwhelming. He found her in her bed, sound asleep. Unable to resist, he went to her. He touched her hair, closed his eyes and drank in the silkiness. She looked so peaceful, so beautiful, asleep in the bed. Despite the tangled mess of black hair on her pillow, she still looked beautiful. Something was different about her. He couldn't place it, but she looked...different. Her skin looked more radiant. Reaching out, he touched her cheek and quickly pulled his hand back when she moaned. He had the most uncontrollable urge to climb into bed with her.

With a deep sigh he left her in her bed, asleep.

The ache in his heart was a heavy one.

Missy woke just as Draco stepped up to the door. She stayed silent as he left.

Had she run from one monster only to land at the doorstep

of one even more hideous? Draco put Ronald's shortcomings to shame. But the way she felt now, she didn't have the strength to run. She barely had the strength to sit up. What she needed was to talk to someone, to cry on someone's shoulder. Lifting the telephone, she dialed. She needed her family, desperately.

When her sister answered the phone, Missy felt her heart ache.

"Hello."

"Trisha, it's Jo." How odd it felt to use her real name.

"Jo, oh God, it's good to hear from you. Where are you? How are you?"

There was no way she could tell her sister where she was for fear Ronald would find out. She didn't have the strength to deal with him now. "You know, don't you?"

"That you left Ronald, yes." She paused. "He says you ran off with another man."

Missy let out an undignified snort. "I left because he threatened to kill me, and nearly succeeded." Missy shook her head. She hadn't meant to say that.

"What? Oh, my God, Jo!"

"It's over. I just wanted to call to tell you I'm okay."

"Jesus, Jo, you can't drop a bombshell like that on me and expect to wash it away like it was nothing."

Missy closed her eyes and wished she hadn't opened that can of worms, not now. "I'm dealing with it, Trisha, in my own way."

"Well at least tell me where you are."

"I can't, not yet. Just know I'm okay." The tears welled up in her eyes. Missy wanted nothing more than to be held by her big sister, but that wasn't possible. She was ashamed of what she'd let happen to her, ashamed of what Ronald had done to her, had turned her into. She needed time to regroup, to become stronger before she faced her family, and her shame. "I'll keep in touch, sis. I love you." She set the phone down before her sister convinced her to tell her more than she was ready to tell.

With tears rolling down her cheeks, Missy lay in her bed, alone, and wept.

Draco tapped the file on Missy, a woman of many mysteries, he thought, as he drew on his cigarette. He wanted to know more. Closing off all other thoughts, tucking everyone else aside, he drifted deep within himself to find the one person amongst many that he looked for. He found Ronald O'Connor, and stepped back at the anger the man was feeling inside. He could understand the hurt of a man whose fiancé had left him, but the rage he felt from Ronald was far more intense.

Dangerous.

Ronald's soul was ugly, which said a lot coming from a demon straight from the pits of hell. There was so much violence in the man, violence that even Draco himself cringed from. But he didn't push it. It was too risky. He'd probed deeper before, only to have the human teetering on the verge of insanity. So he released his hold of the vile man and drew on his cigarette.

What had possessed such a delicate soul to marry someone so dark? If only he knew what was inside Missy's mind, a mystery that still irritated him.

He needed to see her, to make sure she was resting comfortably. He wondered if she was still asleep. Setting himself down outside her bedroom door, he inched it open to see that she was. She wouldn't know if he sat with her while she slept, so what harm could it possibly do? She looked so peaceful in sleep, so enchanting. "Who are you," he asked silently, "and why can't I stay away from you?"

Standing over her, desperate to touch her, he watched her sleep. Dressed in the white robe, her black hair such a stark contrast, she looked so serene. A goddess with wavy hair and eyes as gold as the sun, beneath heavily closed lids, slumbered.

It baffled him why her mind was locked, unable for him to

penetrate. Even in her sleeping state, he felt blocked off from her thoughts. Everything about her intrigued him, and he wanted her with an intensity that ached.

Risking it, he reached a hand out to touch hers and felt that familiar tingle, only this time it seemed less bothersome. What was that sensation and why did he feel it only with her? And why did he want her so badly it hurt? Relaxing in his chair, he watched as she slept, and wished desperately that he could touch his lips to hers, feel her beneath him.

CHAPTER EIGHT

Missy rolled over with a contented sigh, and her eyes slowly fluttered open. She felt great, absolutely marvelous. The previous sickness she'd felt was gone, much to her relief. Unfortunately, the memories still lingered. She'd witnessed something so hideous, so awful, that no horror movie could compare. But she didn't want to think of that now. She was better; it was time to move on, and quickly.

Pushing from the mattress, she turned and saw the chair beside the bed. A flash, like a zap of electricity shot through her mind, shaking her, causing her to stumble back. Draco had sat there, watching while she slept. She could see it as clearly as if he were there now. She shivered, blinked her eyes several times, before brushing it aside.

The energy that soared through her body was incredible. She felt high, invigorated. Where was all this energy coming from? She'd never felt anything like it before in her life.

Stripping out of her robe, she stepped into the shower and started the water.

It was time to leave. She couldn't very well stay in a home owned by a monster. She needed to get out while she still could. But to walk out in broad daylight seemed rather risky. What if Draco saw her leaving? Would he let her go? No, it was best if she waited for darkness, wait until everyone was fast asleep, before making her escape.

How familiar was this? She'd fled another man once before in the darkness of night. Fled for her life, fearing for her life. Now, it seemed she would do it all over again.

Wiping the steam from the mirror, she looked at the reflection that stared back at her with wide eyes. Her skin was no longer pale, instead it seemed to glow with a shade of bronze she hadn't had before. Did her eyes seem darker, a deeper shade of gold? Impossible. They were no different from two days ago.

Glancing at her neck, Missy noticed the wound was nearly gone, leaving barely a scar behind. Lifting her hand to the spot that had once been red with infection from a cut induced by her fiancé she felt only smooth skin, as if nothing had happened to her. Then she saw her arm, and like her neck, there remained only the slightest trace of a wound. How odd that she'd healed so perfectly, in only days. Her wounds disappearing almost as if they'd never occurred.

Baffled, she began to dress. She'd never healed so quickly before. Wasn't that a nice change? Running the brush through her long dark hair, she thought for a second that it shimmered more than usual.

Humming to herself, she set the brush down and stepped from the room. She nearly jumped out of her skin when she saw the housekeeper by her bed. Her hand clamped onto the door handle and it snapped like a frail twig.

"You've broken the door!"

Missy looked down at her hand, the handle still in her grasp. "I...it must have been loose." There was no other explanation for it, but she still felt terrible about it.

The housekeeper held out her hand, palm up. "It wasn't loose yesterday."

Missy dropped the handle into her hand and stared at it with confusion. "I'll pay for the damages." It had to have been flawed. How else could it have snapped so easily when she'd grabbed it?

"No need, the master will have it repaired. Is there anything I can get for you?"

Her eyes still on the door, Missy mumbled her response. "No thank you, I'm fine."

"I'll start cleaning your room. Breakfast is being served in the dining hall."

Missy tore her eyes from the door, nodded lightly at the maid before heading out. How could she have snapped a steel handle without any effort whatsoever? It was impossible, the door must have been flawed. Maybe a crack in the metal.

The dining room was quiet except for a few early birds. Grabbing a plate, Missy began heaping food from an assortment of dishes available from the steaming buffet. She suddenly felt ravenous.

"You're up early. Feeling better?"

Missy turned to Deb, politeness rearing, she smiled. "Yes I am, thank you." How did she know she'd been sick?

"That's a relief. Everyone's been so worried." Deb began filling her own plate. "With you being down with the flu and Jennifer up and leaving—"

"Jennifer left?" Missy interrupted and looked at Deb with wide eyes.

"Yeah, a few nights ago. Packed her bags and up and left. Can't say I'm sorry to see her go. She was beginning to get on my nerves."

Jennifer hadn't left. The memory came up and grabbed hold with a vengeance, making her dizzy. Jennifer had been killed. By Draco.

"Missy? You okay, girl?"

"What?"

"You look really pale. Maybe you should sit down."

"Yeah." She swallowed the bile rising in her throat. "No, I..." She trailed off as she set her plate down.

"You not gonna eat that?"

Missy felt her stomach roll. "No." Quickly, she hurried from the room, running as fast as she could up the stairs and straight for her suite. Once behind the confines of her door, she let out a labored breath. Jennifer hadn't left. She'd been murdered by Draco. The knock at her door nearly made her squeal. Her breath panting, she reached for the knob. As she pulled the door open, she came face to face with a murderer.

"Missy, I heard a rumor that you were up and about." He waltzed into the room, looking as regal as ever in yet another dark suit. "Does that mean you are feeling better?" He turned to face her and his brows drew together. "You're not feeling better, are you? You shouldn't be up."

He stepped toward her. She took a step back.

"I felt fine, or I thought I did. I just needed some food." He looked so handsome, so normal. She knew what hid beneath. Yet, aside from the repulsion, she felt desire. How was that possible? "I guess I just wasn't ready to be up and about yet."

"I'll have a maid bring you your meals."

"I think that would be for the best until I'm feeling better." Until she left.

"A few days of rest and you'll be as good as new."

Oh, his smile was charming, she thought, and had her pulse racing. "I hope so."

"I'll inform my staff." He headed for the door.

"Draco, where is Jennifer?" she asked, surprised by her boldness.

He turned back slowly, his face sober. "She decided this wasn't what she wanted after all and left a few nights ago."

Oh, he was such a good liar. "Odd, isn't it, that she would just up and leave, without telling anyone?" She took a step closer, daringly. "Including me, her friend."

"Well, it's possible she didn't want to disturb you, being that you were sick."

Good comeback, she thought. "Still...seems odd."

"Yes, well, I'll leave you to rest now." Turning, he left, closing the door behind him.

Where had this newfound boldness come from, she

wondered. She'd never been so direct before. To think, she'd just challenged a monster and come out of it unscathed. Baffled by her new strength, Missy stepped out onto the balcony and took in the wonderful morning. She would miss the beauty of this place, the serenity of it, but it was time to leave. Tonight she would be gone.

Missy waited until well after dark before she slipped away. The house was silent, all the occupants fast asleep in their beds after their usual evening stargazing class. She'd attended, biding her time until she was ready to leave. Pulling the French doors open in the sitting room, she stepped out into the cool dark night. A light rain had come early in the evening and now, under the full moon, the damp grass glittered. She stepped outside, and drew in the glorious scent of the lawns and fresh rain.

The energy she'd felt during the day had not dissipated. If anything, she was even more invigorated. Her pack slung over her shoulder, Missy darted from the house and to the yard that spread out behind it. She'd figured it was best to leave out the back rather than from the front. Less likely she'd be caught leaving from the cover of the backyard, with all of its trees and shrubbery. Where she was going, however, she wasn't sure. She would go wherever her feet took her.

Voices in the darkness startled her. She ducked for cover behind a set of tall bushes and could only make out shadows. From the sound of it, there were two of them, both men, and they sounded angry. Realizing she couldn't very well walk past them, Missy decided to head back to the house and go around to the front. Sliding out from behind the cover of the trees, she started for the house. She heard a loud snap as something ripped into her shoulder. She went down hard. The damp ground pressed to her cheek as she fell. The sharp, stabbing sensation was blinding and she had no idea what was happening to her. Swallowing the pain, Missy fought to gain her footing, and stumbled toward the house. Through blurred vision, she saw someone coming toward her.

"Missy?"

"I...need help." She fell against Troy, panting.

"What happened?" He hoisted her up, one arm slung around her waist.

"My shoulder..."

"Let me see...what the hell? You've been shot."

"I don't feel well..."

"No shit!"

"What's going on—? Missy!"

Though his voice sounded hollow, Missy recognized it as Draco's. "No...no, leave me alone," she pleaded. The air around her spun. Then it all went black.

"I just came out here to see what that noise was and found her stumbling toward me."

"I was alerted to the sound as well. It's being investigated."

Troy swallowed. "I think she's been—"

"Ill. I know. What the devil was she doing out here and why does she have her pack on?" Worry filling him, Draco pulled Missy from Troy's grip, and transported them to her room. He laid her on the bed, slipping the pack away and letting it fall to the floor. Troy entered moments later, panting from an obvious race up the stairs.

He called Hunter with his mind as he pulled the blankets over Missy.

"I think she might have been leaving," Troy explained as he inched toward the bed. "Did you see her—"

"You called, sir?" Hunter asked, materializing in the room.

"Missy collapsed outside. I believe she was attempting to leave."

"I found her. I think she's been sh—"

"That will be all now, Troy."

"But—"

Draco sent him away and returned his attention to Missy. "She is still too weak to be on her own. What possessed her to leave in the dead of night?"

"Should I ask around to see if anyone knew why she decided to leave?"

"No, no, it will only arouse suspicions." Unable to resist the need to touch her hair, Draco reached out, slid his hand over the satiny black strands and felt a warm, liquid sensation fill him, one he had never felt before. "She's an interesting creature, don't you think, Hunter?"

"Yes sir, she is indeed."

Draco toyed with her hair, intrigued by its texture and the warmth it brought him. "What would compel a young female to leave a man she is betrothed to?" He turned to Hunter. "Have you any idea?"

"Her relationship might have been troubled."

"True, but why would she have fled with only the barest essentials?" He'd been informed by his maids of the lack of supplies Missy had with her. It was obvious that she'd left in a hurry. What would cause her to run away, and change her name?

Hunter rubbed his chin. "Perhaps she feared her fiancé."

Draco's fingers twined in her hair. "When I did a mind search for Ronald O'Connor, I sensed a great deal of rage, anger and violence. She could very well have been afraid of him." The thought of someone hurting her infuriated him. Another unusual feeling.

"She hasn't spoken to you of him?"

"No, she tells me nothing of her real life." He was simply captivated by her. "That doesn't explain why she decided to leave here so late in the night."

Draco turned to Hunter, shock written all over his face at the thoughts that were rolling around in the man's brain. He heard them as clearly as if Hunter had spoken them aloud. *If I didn't know better, I would say you've fallen for her.*

"Oh, go away, Hunter, and take that overactive brain of yours with you." With a flick of his wrist, Hunter was gone, along with his impertinent thoughts.

Draco could tune the meanderings of the brain off when he chose, but at times, when his guard was down, or he was fatigued, the thoughts of others overcrowded him. Hunter's had seemed to take up permanent residence. He hadn't fallen for Missy. It was impossible for him to be in love with a human. Hunter didn't know what he was talking about. Brushing it off, Draco pulled up a chair and sat while Missy slept.

CHAPTER NINE

Her eyes heavy, Missy fought the sleep still trying to drag her under. Finally, with great effort, she opened her eyes.

"You're awake. I've been so worried."

Draco's presence startled her and made her heart race. She looked to her left just as he stood up from the chair that was placed near the foot of her bed.

"How are you feeling?" He sat down beside her.

"I'm fine." Sitting up, she looked around and saw that it was daylight. The last thing she remembered was being outside, in the dark. And something sharp had stung her shoulder.

"You certainly didn't look fine last night. Why were you leaving?"

Her eyes met his and she thought she saw concern in them. "It was time for me to go."

"Nonsense, you're still too weak to be on your own."

"I'm fine." She couldn't explain why she felt so...off.

"Your shirt is torn. I'll have the maid get you a new one."

Glancing down, seeing the tear on the shoulder of the shirt she'd worn the night before, Missy was reminded of the pain that had seared into her arm as she'd attempted to leave. Everything after that was a total blank. "How did I get back here?"

"I brought you to your room after Troy and I found you outside. You're welcome to stay here as long as you like."

She watched him twist the gold and emerald ring on his right hand. Was he nervous? "It's time I moved on."

"I thought you wanted to know all there was to know about the stars?"

"I can learn all I need to know from books."

The smile filled his handsome face. "I suppose that's true enough, but not as much fun as lying out in the dark and gazing up at them."

"And how would you know about that? I have yet to see you attend any one of the sessions we've had since coming here," she challenged, once again surprising herself with her boldness.

"I know all there is to know of the stars. That's what I have instructors for, to teach you."

"Benefits of the founder I suppose?" She smoothed out her hair, suddenly feeling very rumpled in his presence.

His eyes twinkled with amusement. "Naturally. Well, I should let you rest." He tucked his hands in the pockets of his trim black pants. "I'll have the maid bring you breakfast."

She tipped her head in acknowledgement and watched him leave. She understood the dark suits now. Dark colors for a dark force. And it fit him so well, made him look even more intriguing, and yes, handsome.

She shook that thought away. Why she was attracted to him was beyond her. Only thing she could figure out was that she had a habit of falling for dangerous men.

Sliding from the bed, her legs a little wobbly, she managed to walk to the washroom. What she needed was a nice hot shower. But no sooner had she stepped beneath the spray did she realize it hadn't been the smartest move. With the room spinning, she shut the water off, wrapped a towel around her body, and sat down on the toilet. Breathing through the dizziness, she slipped into her cotton nightgown, leaving the four buttons down the front open. She didn't have the strength to do them up. With her hair still soaking wet, she stumbled back to her bed and had just climbed beneath the covers when there was a knock on her door.

"Come in." She needed to fight off whatever was making her so sick so she could get out of this place.

"Hey, how's it going?"

Seeing Troy brought a flash of a memory from the night before. Had he been there? "Not bad," she responded and pulled the covers up a little higher.

"You look kinda green. No pun intended. You sure you're okay?"

"Just feeling a little wobbly. Hey, were you outside last night?"

He sat at the foot of the bed, the very same place Draco had sat moments earlier. "Yep. I was the one that caught you when you fell. How's the shoulder?"

She remembered now. She'd stumbled toward him, he'd caught her. "Sore."

"I imagine so. I'm assuming Draco got his doctor to patch you up."

Completely baffled, she frowned with her response. "I have no idea what you're talking about."

He pointed to his left shoulder, before pointing to hers. "You were shot last night. I wonder if Draco knows who did it."

"I wasn't shot." What was he talking about?

"Yes, you were. I saw it clear as day. On your left shoulder."

She looked down at her shoulder, pulled her nightshirt out to get a glimpse beneath the cloth and was shocked to see a small red hole on her skin. "What the—how did I get that?"

"Ummm, a bullet. Wow, that sure healed up fast. Wait—"

Releasing her shirt, she glared at Troy. "I wasn't shot."

"Oh, yes you were. Trust me, I know what a bullet wound looks like."

"I think you need to leave." She couldn't have been shot...yet the wound...the pain....

"Come on. You can't tell me you're oblivious. How else

would you have that wound?"

"I don't know, but I certainly wasn't shot. I would have felt—"

"A blinding pain that made you dizzy and caused you to black out? Sound familiar?"

It did, still..."I think you should leave."

"No one heals that fast, well, almost no one unless you're—Holy hell! You're the one!"

He was really beginning to piss her off. "Now what are you talking about?"

He jumped off the bed so quickly it startled her. "You're the one he's been looking for. Holy fuck! You're a demon."

"I am not!" Climbing out of the bed, she walked to the door, yanking it open. "Get out!" He grabbed her arm and she threw him across the room. Standing there in shock, Missy had no idea where her sudden strength had come from. "Oh, my God! Are you okay?"

He got to his feet, straightened his shirt. "Wanna tell me again that you're not a demon? Shit. Does Draco know?"

"No. He can't know—I mean—"

"You know what he is! Holy fuck! This is great. He is going to flip when I tell him."

She ran to him, grabbing him by both arms. "You can't tell him." What was she saying? Releasing him, she took a deep breath. "None of this makes sense. I need you to leave."

"It all makes perfect sense. A bullet wound to your shoulder that heals up within hours. Your strength. You're the one he's looking for. How did it happen? Or have you known your entire life you're a demon?"

"I'm not a demon, Troy, and you'd better stop saying that before I get really mad."

He held his hands up. "I'm an innocent party here, just trying to help. At any time did Draco start talking to you in a weird foreign language?"

Her eyes went wide.

"He did!"

"No, not to me. To Jennifer. He killed her!" She gasped, stumbled back.

"He performed the ritual on Jennifer? I guess she didn't leave after all. I kinda thought that was weird. He killed her, you say. How?"

How could he be so nonchalant about murder? "Did you not hear what I said? He killed her. Murdered her!"

Troy waved a hand at her statement. "He's done that before. So how the hell did the incantation work on you?"

She couldn't believe him. He was acting as if murder was nothing more than...breathing. "I was in the room when he killed her."

"Holy sh—wait. How is that possible? That Draco doesn't know you're the one?"

"You keep saying that, and I have no idea what you're talking about. I was hiding in a closet when he and Jennifer came into his office." The room began to spin. "I don't feel so good." She sat down on the bed and lowered her head.

She felt Troy sit down beside her.

"Wow, this is so incredible." A bubble of laughter spurted out. "He's been looking for you for years."

Lifting her head, she looked at him with utter confusion. "What are you talking about?"

"You're the Halfling. A child born from a demon and human. Everyone assumed you'd been killed before birth, but Draco heard you were alive. As soon as he heard that, he started searching for you."

She didn't understand what he was talking about and she didn't care. She felt like crap and just wanted him to leave. "I asked you to leave. Now, you either go willingly or I call someone to escort you from my room."

"Okay, okay. I'm outta here. Think about what I said." He stood, hands held up. "Looks like breakfast is being served."

He left and a tall, thin brown-haired woman in a maid's uniform entered her room with a tray of steaming hot eggs and sausage. Missy thanked her and waited until she left to start eating. Despite her hunger, her mind wandered to her shoulder and the wound on it. There was no way Troy could be right, was there? She wasn't a demon. Was everyone in this place nuts?

She needed to get out, and now.

Setting the tray of half-eaten food aside, Missy climbed from the bed. Grabbing a navy dress from the closet—when had her belongings been put away?—she slipped it on and began stuffing her clothes back into her pack. She needed to go, *now*. It didn't matter that it was still early, or that she still felt weak; she needed to go. And no one, no one was going to stop her.

As she tugged the door open, she came face to face with Draco.

"Well, don't you look refreshed. Much better than the last time I saw you." He reached up to touch her cheek and once again she stepped back.

She stuffed the pack behind the door. "I'm feeling better, thank you." She wasn't a demon. She wasn't like Draco.

"I'm glad to hear that. Can we talk for a moment?" Without waiting for an answer, he simply strolled into the room and planted himself on the sofa.

Make yourself at home, she thought bitterly as she closed the door. Did he have to look so good when she desperately wanted him to be the hideous creature she knew him to be? It would make it so much easier to hate him. "I suppose so."

"Fabulous." He gave her a coy smile. "I was curious; you never gave me an answer as to why you were leaving."

Because she figured he wasn't going away anytime soon, she decided to take a seat rather than stand. "I wasn't aware I needed to answer to you."

"You don't, not to me at least." He rested his arm casually on the back of the sofa. "Perhaps you were going back to your fiancé?"

"I don't have a fiancé." She swallowed the lie.

"Oh, I know, Missy Green is single." He made a gesture with his hands. "But Joanne Morrow is very much engaged."

She wet her lips. Her mouth suddenly felt dry as a bone.

"How did you find that out?"

"I have my ways." Pulling the gold case from his pocket, he slid a cigarette out and slowly flicked the lighter to the tip. "Why did you run?" The tip of the cigarette glowed red as he drew in.

"I had my reasons." The cold lick of steel on her skin had been the reason. "Have you contacted him yet?"

"Why would I do that?" Slowly, he took a long pull from his cigarette while his eyes stayed locked to hers. "Unless you would like me to?"

"No!" The panic rose up and took hold. He couldn't, not now, not ever. If he did, she'd be dead.

"All right, he need not know."

"Thank you."

"Why are you afraid of your fiancé?" Standing, he walked to the bar and poured them each a glass of something from the glass decanter on her mini bar.

"I'm not afraid of my fiancé," she lied.

"Your earlier protest proves differently." He held the glass out to her.

She took the glass. Looking up at him, she felt herself drawn into his eyes.

"He hurt you?"

She let out a sigh as she stared down into the glass. "Yes." What was the point in denying it, now that he knew who she really was?

"He was physical with you?"

She took a sip, surprised at the smooth flavor. Normally she didn't drink alcohol, but whatever was in her glass went down quite easily. "Depends what you consider physical."

"He was brutal with you?" He set his cigarette in the glass ashtray on the coffee table.

What the hell, he already knew everything. Why not go for the gusto? "Would you consider slicing into a woman's flesh with knives brutal? If so, then yes, he was." What Draco might consider brutal was beyond her: he had slaughtered a woman for no apparent reason.

The glass shattered in his hand.

"Oh my! Are you all right?" She jumped up, reaching out to his hand only to have him yank it away.

"I'm fine." He jumped up, grabbed a napkin from the bar and wiped the liquid from his hand. "Your fiancé took a knife to you?"

"Knives, plural, and yes, several times." She downed the contents of her drink in one swallow. She had no idea why she felt the need to suddenly let it out, but she did. "He attacked me. Held a knife to my throat. I ran. I knew if I didn't, he'd kill me." Her hand came up and she could've sworn she felt the cold steel against her skin. "Finding your bus was very convenient at the time."

"He cut your throat?" he gasped.

How could a man—thing—like Draco be capable of disgust at the act of slicing into flesh? Missy wasn't too sure, but he certainly looked appalled. "You look shocked, Draco. Haven't you ever heard of Sadism?"

"I'm familiar with the term." He walked back to the sofa, put out his cigarette. "Your fiancé derived pleasure from inflicting pain on you."

She angled her head and leaned on one hip. That was such a nice way to put it. She chose the nasty form instead. "He got off on cutting me. It's a sick sexual act that I would prefer not to have to relive ever again."

"I'm sorry."

The emotion in his voice surprised her. "Are you?"

"Of course I am. No one should have to endure such atrocities."

She nearly mentioned that what he had done to Jennifer was far worse than what she'd endured at Ronald's hands, but she kept silent. "Yes, well, now you know why I ran, why I lied about who I was."

"You made the right decision. Why did you not run to your family?"

"It's complicated and I don't really feel like getting into it now." What would he know about shame? She was sure he felt none. If he did, he wouldn't be able to hold his head up after what he'd done to Jennifer.

He nodded. "Have you contacted your family yet?"

How much did he know about her she wondered? "Only once." She let out a long heavy sigh. She didn't want to think of her family. She missed them too much. "If you don't mind, I'd rather not get into any more right now."

"All right, I will leave you for now." He headed to the door, paused, before turning. "You're safe here, Missy." He closed the door behind him with a quiet click.

A bubble of laughter slipped through her lips. "Safe, here? I hardly think so." Dropping her head onto the back of the sofa, she let out a long sigh. That short conversation had drained her. Who was she kidding? She wasn't strong enough to leave. As much as she wanted to run, she wouldn't get far.

CHAPTER TEN

Missy chose a book from the library. With a sigh, she decided she needed some quiet time alone to relax and recuperate and forget, even just for a moment, all that had happened in the past few days.

Missy didn't want to think about Draco, who he was, what he was, and what he had done. She didn't want to think about Ronald and all the things he'd done to her in the years they'd been together. And she certainly didn't want to think about what Troy had babbled to her.

For now, she wanted to relax.

She slipped back into her robe and curled up on the bed with a Danielle Steele novel. She'd never read a romance novel, but this particular book caught her eye and she decided to give it a chance.

"Knock, knock." Troy stuck his head in the door, a wide smile on his face.

So much for being alone. Missy pulled her legs down, adjusted her robe, and gestured for him to come in.

"I thought I would come by and see how you were doing." He sat down on the edge of the bed.

Uncomfortable with him being so close to her, she shifted away. "You don't have to keep checking up on me, Troy. I'm fine."

"Actually, I have an ulterior motive."

"I'm not interested in you that way, Troy."

The smile that rose on his lips added a boyish charm to his face. "I won't say I'm not disappointed, but that's not what I was going to say. Have you told Draco that you're the one yet?"

"The one what?"

"The demon he's been looking for."

She set her book on the nightstand. "I'm not a demon, Troy and I wish you would just leave me alone."

"I thought you'd come to your senses by now. Okay, time to prove to you who you really are."

She saw the glint of steel barely a second before his hand jutted out. She felt the slash to her leg a second later. She screamed, yanked her leg back, and instantly pressed her hand to the wound. Memories of Ronald cutting her came back with a nasty blow.

"Stop it!" she bellowed, trying to catch her breath.

"Move your hand." Grabbing her wrist, Troy yanked her hand away from her leg. "Where's the blood, Missy? For that matter, look at the wound. It's healing already."

"I told you to get out!"

"Just look, damn it!"

Her heart and pulse racing, she glanced down and was surprised that there was no blood. Not only that, the wound seemed to be sealing itself.

"And what about your shoulder? I bet that's completely gone by now." He yanked the robe from her shoulder.

She slapped his hand away and tugged her robe back in place. Her earlier wound was gone, but that didn't mean anything.

"How can you be so dense?"

"Watch it!"

"You're a demon."

"Okay. That's it. Get out!" Before her eyes, Troy vanished. One minute he was standing before her, the next he was gone.

She blinked her eyes in confusion. "Troy?" Sliding off the bed, she hurried into her sitting room. He wasn't there either. She jumped when the door flew open and Troy rushed into the room.

"You sent me outside. It's pouring out there." His hair and clothing were soaking wet.

A bubble of laughter slipped out, surprising her. He looked so funny dripping wet and angry.

"That wasn't nice."

She calmed herself. "Where did you go?"

"I just said. You sent me outside."

"How could I have sent you outside?" He wasn't making any sense.

"With your mind. You have powers, like the ability to send people anywhere you choose. You can send yourself anywhere as well. Look, can I get a towel?"

Baffled by what he was saying, Missy waited while he grabbed a towel from her washroom. "It's physically impossible for me to have *sent* you anywhere."

He came back into the room, rubbing the towel over his hair. "Yeah, explain how I disappeared?"

"You must have run from my room." He simply stared at her with a *get real* sort of look. Okay, that did sound flimsy, even to her. "I'm not a demon."

"Sure. Okay. And I'm not a man. Wake up and smell the coffee, babe. You are a demon. How's your leg?"

She looked down and all she saw was a thin red line.

"Being a demon is pretty fucking awesome. You can have anything you want with merely a thought. If you don't feel like getting dressed in the morning, just think of what you want to wear and poof! You're dressed. Why walk to the kitchen if you're hungry or thirsty? Just think it and you've got it. What more could a person ask for?"

She dropped down on the sofa. Her mind reeling.

"Have you read anyone's mind yet?"

She looked up, met his gaze. "Pardon?"

"You can read minds. Try reading mine." He sat down on the coffee table across from her.

"Don't be silly." She didn't have the ability to read minds.

I would love to strip you out of that bathrobe and get a mouthful of those gorgeous tits!

"You pig!"

He clapped his hands together, making her jump. "Yes! You read what I was thinking. Just so you know, I really would like to jump you."

She got to her feet, furious. "It's time you left."

"I'm great in bed. Ask anyone."

Appalled by his boldness, she slapped her hands to his shoulders. She gave him a hard shove, sending him flying across the room. "Oh, Lord! I am so sorry. Are you all right?"

He got to his feet, laughing. "You are a hell of a woman. If you change your mind and want to give Troy a try, just call me with your mind and I'll come running."

Her jaw dropped as he left the room. The man was unbelievable. Shaking him out of her thoughts, she headed to the shower. Dropping the robe on the floor, she set the temperature, and stepped underneath the streaming water. She lathered up, rubbing the soft fragrant soap all over her body. When she reached the spot on her leg where Troy had cut and saw the thin red seam already fading, she paused. How could she have healed so quickly? And why hadn't she bled? She wasn't a demon. Was she?

She washed her hair, rinsed off, and stepped out of the shower.

Straightening, she leaned toward the mirror and examined her neck. The cut she'd received from Ronald wasn't even visible. Glancing at her shoulder, the wound that had been there the day before was now gone. She lifted her wrist and frowned, as that wound was also gone. She'd never healed that fast before. How was it possible she did now?

She wasn't a demon.

Drying off, she hung the damp towels over the rack before

heading to her suite to change. Grabbing a light button-up shirt, she left the top three undone. There was no need to cover up now, since everything had healed. And Ronald wasn't around to tell her to do them all up. Pulling her hair back, she tied it in a ponytail, dabbed on the eyeliner and mascara she'd hidden in her bag. She felt oddly refreshed. Hopefully the flu, or whatever had struck her so violently, was gone.

She noticed the door handle was now repaired. That incident still baffled her. How could she have broken the knob so easily? It snapped so perfectly, like it had no consistency. Shaking it off, she headed out to her suite just as someone knocked on her door. Hoping it wasn't Troy again, she opened it with a bit of reluctance. She was surprised to see Hunter on the other side.

"Hello, Miss. Draco wishes me to invite you to his suite for dinner."

"Oh, well..." She didn't want to be impolite, but she wasn't really in the mood for more company.

"He's already prepared the meal. He doesn't take no lightly." Hunter prodded.

No, she imagined he didn't. "I guess the answer is yes."

"May I escort you?"

"Now?"

He nodded and held out his elbow.

Frowning, Missy took hold of his arm and closed her door as she left. She took a few deep calming breaths as Hunter escorted her to Draco's suite.

He knocked once, pushed the door open, and held a hand out for her to enter. She took another deep breath and stepped inside.

"Missy, wonderful of you to join me." Draco held his hand out to show her inside.

She smiled politely as she walked into the room. He'd set a table near the window, complete with candles that glittered in the dim light. Something about him always seemed to pull at her, and it wasn't the most comfortable feeling.

Once again, he wore black, only this time he'd omitted the jacket. He looked very dapper, she thought, for a demon that is.

"Please, have a seat." He held the chair for her.

Why had she never noticed how good he smelled before? It wasn't a scent she recognized, not that she was good enough with men's colognes that she would know one from the other. But it was enticing to say the least.

"I hope you like steak? I've had the cook prepare two thick sirloins for us."

"Steak is fine." She sat down, smoothing out her skirt as he walked around the table to his seat.

"Perfect. How would you like it cooked?"

"Rare." She smiled at Hunter as he stood dutifully, waiting by the table. The poor guy always looked so nervous.

"Ah, a lady after my own tastes." He gave her a generous smile as he turned to Hunter. "Two steaks, rare."

Why she'd chosen the rare steak was beyond her. She normally preferred her meat well-cooked. "He always looks so stiff. Hunter," she explained softly to Draco when he gave her a puzzled look.

"He's the nervous type. It is so good to see color in your cheeks. I was beginning to get rather worried about you."

"I'm touched by your concern, but it isn't necessary." She lifted the glass of water set out in front of her and wet her parched throat.

"Have you called your father or siblings yet?" He blew out a stream of cloudy smoke overhead as he kept his eyes on her.

"I called my sister. You're pretty thorough, aren't you?" She looked up at him and their eyes met, held, and she felt her pulse race. He was a handsome man, there was no doubt about that. Still...

"I believe in being thorough. Did you tell your sister where you are staying?"

"No." She swirled her glass, her eyes captivated by his. So dark, so very dark.

"Why not?"

"Because I don't want them calling Ronald." She felt the strangest sensations fill her at his steady stare. Almost as if she should surrender her soul to him, to give in and let him have her. For one brief second, she wanted to.

"You think they'll tell him where you are?"

"No, but they'll try to encourage me to come home." She wasn't ready yet, she wasn't strong enough yet.

He lifted the cigarette and drew on it. "You don't want that?" he said and the smoke trailed from his lips as he spoke.

"No." She lifted her water and sipped. "I'm not ready yet." She couldn't face their questions, possible accusations, the 'I told you not to marry so young.' Her family loved her and were concerned for her, she knew that, and she knew just as well that they had been right. Another reason why she found it hard to face them.

"Are you not close with your brothers and sister?"

"We're close enough. What else did you find out about me?"

Smiling, he lounged in his chair, lifting the cigarette casually to his lips. "Everything, including school transcripts. There's quite an intelligent brain behind all the beauty. It's unfortunate that you didn't follow through with higher education, though."

"Do you have everyone investigated that joins your group?" She twisted her napkin into a tiny ball out of agitation. How was it a man that was capable of devouring a human being could be so poised, so debonair and so damn charming?

"Only those who are secretive. It wouldn't be very wise if I didn't research my guests. You lost your mother a few years ago."

"Yes, I did. This seems a bit excessive. I understand you wanting to know who you have staying with you, as in if they have a criminal record, but going that deep is an invasion of privacy."

"I'm sorry. It seems I've touched on a sore spot." He crushed his cigarette out in the ashtray on the table.

"My mother and I were close. Her death was hard on me."

She didn't think he needed to know anything more.

The door opened and Hunter walked in, wheeling a cart with plates of food that smelled absolutely divine. "Bon appetit," he murmured. He removed the ashtray and placed the plates on the table.

"Thank you, Hunter."

He bowed his head as he wheeled the cart from the room.

The poor guy, she thought, always a ball of nerves. "I have to say, the food here is incredible."

"I have a wonderful cook."

"You do at that. I'm surprised you're not fat from all this wonderful food." *Do demons gain weight?* As she cut into her steak, the juices seeped from the meat, arousing her appetite. "Oh," she moaned as she sampled the first bite. "This is incredible."

Angling his head, he gave her a quizzical look.

"What?" She dabbed the napkin to her mouth in case any juices had dribbled onto her chin.

"I can't place it, but something is different about you."

She laughed it off and cut into her steak. "I'm still the same person I was when I came here." The juices from the steak had her mouth watering. She felt ravenous, as if she hadn't eaten in days, and craved the combination of meat and bloody juice.

Her hand froze at her lips; the fork fell to the plate with a crash.

"Is everything all right?"

She looked up at him, her eyes wide. Recognition was a hard slap to the face and right now, hers was on fire. "No...I...no. I need to go." Pushing from the table, she rushed to the door.

What have I done to make her leave so quickly?

She spun on him, his words as clear to her as if he'd spoken them aloud. "What did you just say?"

"I asked if everything was all right." *She doesn't look well. Perhaps I should call the doctor.*

His thoughts were screaming out at her. Terrified at her

revelation, she grabbed the door and ran to her room. She burst inside, slamming the door behind her, and paced the floor.

Blood. She had craved the blood of that steak. Not just craved, desperately needed to have it. Not to mention, she'd read his mind. Stared right at his face and heard his thoughts so clearly yet his lips never moved. She'd heard Troy's thoughts as well.

She wasn't a demon.

Was she?

Running for the mini-bar, she grabbed the corkscrew and with a quick intake of breath, stabbed her finger. There was no blood and in a matter of seconds, the wound began to seal itself shut. Hand shaking, she pressed the tip of the foil knife to her palm, and sliced. It burned like hell, but again, there was no blood. She stared at her palm as the cut closed up.

"No, no, this isn't right. This can't be happening." She jumped when the door flew open. Draco strode in.

"Are you all right? What have you done?" He ran to her, knocking the corkscrew from her hand, and dragging her to the sink.

"There's no blood," she murmured as he turned the tap on. "There's no blood!" She demanded and yanked her hand free. "I'm not bleeding. Look!" She held her arm up.

"What the—" His face went white and he stumbled back. "You!"

"I want blood. I hate blood, yet I want it. I can taste it still and I want it so badly I could—" *Kill for it.* She clamped her mouth shut at the thought.

"How? When?"

"Do you bleed?" she asked, dumbfounded.

"No. How did this happen?"

"Troy said it was an incantation you performed on Jennifer. An incantation to bring out the demon. I was in the room when you killed her." Was this really happening or was she dreaming?

He stared at her for several seconds before responding. "How was it you were in the room and I not know it?"

"I was hiding in the closet. I came to thank you for giving me something to do and when you weren't there, I was going to write you a note. I got scared when I heard you coming toward the door. I don't know why, but I was. I thought the door at the back of your office was an exit, but it was a closet. I saw it all. You killed her."

Draco grimaced. "I had to."

"Had to?"

"Her mind snapped. She was as rabid as a wild animal. I knew nothing else to do for her."

"So you killed her? Dear God!"

"It was all I could do. That's why you've been ill. Your body is attempting to change into the demon." He reached out to touch her face and she stepped back.

"Will I look like you?" She wasn't sure she could handle it if she did.

"I really have no idea. You are the only living Halfling."

"What is a halfling?"

"A child of both demon and human origin. I knew you looked different these past few days."

His face was beaming and Missy could actually feel the joy he felt. How odd was that? "What do you mean, I'm the only living...halfling?"

"To mate with a human is taboo. Satan does not allow it and terminates the child before it can be born. We were all under the impression you had been taken care of before birth."

Her chin dropped. Everything he said was shocking. Where did she start? "Satan? As in the Devil?"

"Yes. Oh, this is absolutely marvelous!"

"Marvelous? What the hell is so marvelous? I'm a hideous beast."

"You are beautiful."

She stepped back again when he reached out for her.

"Why do you step away from me every time I try to touch

you?"

"I'm not like you. I will never be like you." She would rather die than be like him.

"I have no idea what you are now. We need to find that out."

She held her hand up, her shoulders squared. "No, we do not. You need to leave."

"There is so much I need to teach you, Missy."

"I don't want you teaching me anything."

"You're afraid. I can understand that, but—"

"Afraid? That's putting it mildly." The laughter bubbled up and she feared if she didn't still it quickly, it would lead to hysterics. "You need to leave. Now!"

"We're not finished."

"Yes, Draco, we are." She grabbed his arm and physically tossed him from her room, which was no easy task given her size in comparison to his. Leaning against the door, she blew out a huge breath.

What had she just done?

CHAPTER ELEVEN

Needing some air, Missy stood on the terrace, looking out at the huge property before her. It ran for miles, open fields of green. To the right she saw a row of shrubs sculpted into animals, dragons, and armored soldiers. Whoever the sculptor was, he was fabulous.

Why did one man—demon—need so much land?

Her head was throbbing something fierce and she wished she had an Advil.

Feeling something in her hand, Missy opened her palm and was shocked to see the round, red pill resting against her skin. She'd wished for it and received it. What she needed was a glass of water to wash it down and in a split second, she held a tall glass of clear, cold water.

She swallowed, hard and stared at the Advil in one hand and the glass in the other. She had made them appear.

She really *was* a demon.

Taking the pill, she washed it down with the water as she sauntered back into her sitting area. Placing the glass on the table, she sat down on the sofa and stared blankly.

What did Troy say? She could have anything she wanted.

"I want chocolate cake." She jumped when a thick dark chocolate two-layer cake landed on her lap. Grabbing the plate before it fell over, she set it on the table and simply stared at it. "Holy hell!" She really could have anything.

Wasn't that just great! Just bloody great!

Jolting at the knock on her door, she debated making the cake disappear. She decided she could just say it was from the kitchen. Wondering who it might be at her door, Missy contemplated not answering it. When the knock sounded again, she let out a long breath, "Enter," she called out halfheartedly. When Troy stepped in, she let out a long sigh. "What do you want now?"

"To see how you're doing." *And to see if you'd changed you mind about sleeping with me.*

"I'm just dandy and no, I haven't changed my mind about sleeping with you. Just leave me alone, Troy." Since the cake was in front of her, she was encouraged to taste it. She wished for a fork, knife, and plate, and when they appeared beside her, she started cutting into the cake.

"Well, looks like you've finally accepted who you are. That's great. Cut me a slice."

He sat down beside her and held out his own plate and fork. "You're a demon, too?"

"Not the same kind as Draco, but yeah. Wow, this looks great." He dug in the instant she laid the slice on his plate.

"There are different types of demons?" What did she know? Up until a week ago she had no idea such things existed.

"Oh sure. Vampires, werewolves, trolls, shape-shifters, just to name a few," he responded through the cake in his mouth.

She cut her own slice and sat back to give it a sample.

"But Draco is the direct descendent of Satan, one of few, which makes him a muckety-muck, so to speak."

"What do you mean a direct descendent?" The cake was pretty good.

"Lucifer is his great-great-great-grandfather."

Missy nearly choked on the cake in her mouth. Troy grabbed the water from the table and held it out to her. She took it and sipped. "Are you serious?" she managed, after catching her breath.

"Perfectly."

"Tell me more about him?"

"Well, as you know, he owns Starr Gazers as well as being CEO and owner of Starr Industries. He's worth billions. Used to collect souls for Satan—"

"Come again?" She took another forkful of cake.

"Satan granted him leave from Hell with the condition he grab souls. But he doesn't do that anymore."

"Well..."

"Does he know about you yet?"

She set the glass on the table. "Yes. I just told him."

"I bet he was out-of-his-mind thrilled! He's finally found his mate."

The fork in her hand paused midway to her mouth. "Excuse me?"

"His mate. You." He gobbled down more cake.

"Why am I his mate?"

"Because you're the only one of your kind."

"So?"

He licked the fork clean. "You'd have to ask Draco that. So I guess I won't be springing the good news on him. Damn, I was hoping for some brownie points."

"Sorry to disappoint you." Having had enough cake, she set it aside, and sat back, arms crossed. "Why me? All I wanted was to get away from Ronald and this is what I get."

"Who is Ronald?" Troy took her plate and finished off her half-eaten slice.

"My fiancé. I need something to drink. Something strong. What's a strong drink?"

"Gin. You're engaged?"

"Was. Unfortunately." In her hand, she held a glass filled halfway with what she could only assume was gin. "I didn't ask for this. I never should have gotten on that bus." She took a sip and nearly choked on it.

"Babe, that was the best thing you could have done."

"I disagree," she choked, catching her breath. "These past few years have been so crappy. All I wanted was a new start."

"And you got that. Stop wallowing. You'll see in no time. Being a demon is pretty awesome."

"Leave me alone, Troy." She envisioned sending him to the shrubs, right near the mouth of the dragon-shaped one, and he was gone, just like that. If he'd actually ended up there, she wasn't sure, and she didn't care.

What was so great about being a demon? Sure, she could have anything she wanted, but so what? She didn't want to be an animal like Draco.

Downing the contents of the glass, she coughed and gasped for air as her body shook. That was the most disgusting liquid she'd ever tasted.

She envisioned her room filled with balloons in various shapes and sizes, hoping it would cheer her up. It didn't. Missy felt miserable. Instead of admiring them, enjoying them, she decided to pop them, one by one, with only a thought.

Here's to life.

Pop!

Here's to having powers.

Pop!

Here's to wishing a lifetime of pain and misery on Ronald and Draco.

Pop, pop, pop, pop!

"Amusing yourself, I see." Draco appeared before her, startling her.

She caught her breath and replied calmly. "I've pictured your face on every one of them— no—that's not true. That one is Ronald." Lifting a finger, she popped the deep green balloon. She still felt miserable.

"Very amusing." He pushed through the many balloons to get to her.

"I think so." Pop, another one down. "So, Draco, to what do I owe the discomfort of your visit this time?" Pop, another one down.

"Aren't we in a foul mood?"

"I am. I don't know about you. Why are you here?" In the blink of an eye, all of the balloons disappeared. "Party pooper."

"I wanted to ask you a few questions."

She turned her head to face him and the room began to swim before her. "Questions, always questions with you. Let me ask you one for a change. Why are you looking for a mate?"

"To share my life with, of course."

"Why me?" Her vision was beginning to blur. Was this what being drunk was like? She'd never been before.

He blinked several times before responding. "You're the only one of your kind."

"And that's it? You want me because I'm rare?"

"I did. Before I knew you. Where is this going, Missy?"

"I'm just curious if love played any part in this search for a mate. See, when I accepted Ronald's proposal, I believed I was in love. I figured we would have a long, happy life together, have a few children, grow old and die together." She looked over at Draco. "Well, that didn't exactly work out, so I was just curious what your idea of happily-ever-after is?"

"I've never really given it any thought."

"Well, I would think that would be something to think about when choosing a mate. However, I really don't know what you feel, being a direct descendent of Satan and all. Can you feel?" she slurred.

"How did you find that out?"

"I have my ways," she responded slyly. "Can you?"

"I didn't come here to be grilled by you."

"I wasn't grilling you. I was just asking questions. What's the matter, Draco? You don't like being questioned?"

He got to his feet. "I think I'll come back when you're in a better mood."

"Oh, don't go. I'm in a perfectly fine mood now, Draco." She swaggered toward him.

"You're drunk."

"Yep, yep I am. Why is it I get the strangest urge to rip those clothes from your body and see what's hidden beneath all that black?" She ran a finger along his lapel. "Yet, at the same time, I want to vomit at your feet."

"What sort of response were you expecting from that question? Or was it a rhetorical one?"

"Yeah, the last one," she slurred.

"This is all new to you. It will take time for you to adjust."

"Oh, I've grasped it all. I'm now a demon who craves flesh and blood and my future is filled with uncertainty, but one thing remains." The tears came up and flooded her eyes despite her fight to withhold them. "I can never go home again."

"Missy."

"No." She waved him off. "Leave me be. I need some time alone."

"You keep pushing me away, yet it's me you need."

"I don't need you." She stepped away and was shocked when he yanked her back toward him. Before she knew it, his mouth was covering hers. She felt the heat scorch her from the middle of her belly and down. Something inside of her beckoned her to surrender.

"I have never wanted a woman's lips before." He ran his thumb over her lips. "Yours tempt me beyond reason." With that said, he vanished.

She slumped to the floor, her eyes flooded with tears.

Now why did he have to do that?

CHAPTER TWELVE

The sun was beginning to rise, producing tints of orange and pink in the sky. Draco stood watch while it all unfolded. It was a beautiful sight, fascinating, and he wished he could watch it with Missy. He'd never felt a need so great before and wasn't quite sure what to do about it. Everything about her pulled at him in a way he'd never experience before. Sure, he'd had women, but they meant nothing more to him than to satisfy a sexual urge. The moment they'd left his bed, they'd left his mind. And he certainly never wanted to kiss any one of them. Yet with Missy, her lips beckoned to him and the instant he'd touched them with his own he'd felt an explosion of desire fill him. Not entirely sexual, he mused, but something more. Something deeper.

Her comment hurt him, another thing he wasn't used to. He was a confident man and held no care for what others thought of him for the most part. He was stronger than any mere human, after all. Still, hearing Missy say she felt like vomiting at the sight of him hurt.

He heard Hunter enter, but didn't turn to greet him.

"Sir, can I get you anything?"

"I've finally found her, Hunter."

"Oh, that's wonderful, sir! Who might she be?"

"Missy." It was all supposed to be so easy. He would perform the incantation to bring forth his mate, take her into his life, teach her the ways of being a demon, and live the rest of his days with her as his woman. Now, he worried none of his plan would come to fruition. Missy had been so cold, so distant.

"Well, isn't that a pleasant surprise."

"She saw me kill that young woman a few days ago. Jennifer."

"I see."

Draco picked at the imaginary lint on his slacks. "She was repulsed."

"Well, sir, it is hard for the average person to grasp."

Draco lifted his eyes to Hunter. "You manage."

Hunter shrugged his shoulders. "I've been with you for decades. She's never experienced such a thing before."

"The first time, were you repulsed?" He suddenly wanted to know, not knowing why now it seemed so important.

Hunter paused. "I was shocked." *I was repulsed.*

Draco sighed. When would he ever learn? "You were disgusted, Hunter, just admit it. You tend to forget I can read your thoughts."

Hunter bowed his head. "Yes, sir."

"Was that a yes to the disgust, or yes to your forgetting I can read minds?"

"Yes, sir."

Draco let out a chuckle that had Hunter's eyes coming up. "Okay, we will leave it at that." He rose and walked to the window. It was difficult for him to understand the workings of the human mind. What repulsed one didn't always repulse another.

"Give her time, sir. She will come around." Hunter turned and walked, stiff as ever, to the door. "I did," he said as he left.

Draco smiled as he watched Hunter through the window. Yes, Hunter had come around, quite nicely, and he really should treat him better. The man was incredibly loyal, so he wasn't always the most intelligent, but he was faithful. And he'd been with Draco through many years of ups and downs. He was the closest thing to a friend Draco had. Letting out a sigh, Draco watched the day come to light.

When he saw her outside his window, his body came alive.

Too restless to sleep, Missy decided to wander the yard and see just how far the property actually went. She'd spent hours tossing in bed before deciding to give up. Her mind was too active to sleep. In the course of an hour, her life had changed drastically. She was no longer human. Tough to sleep with that revelation stirring in your head.

With the sun just beginning to rise, the yard was cast in a hue of red that was eerie yet oddly beautiful. Her nose tickled with all the new fragrances in the air. She'd noticed her senses had become more acute, more sensitive. Things felt better, smelled better, tasted better. Even the ordinary seemed extraordinary. Was the sunrise always so beautiful? Were the trees always so tall and full? Was the grass always this soft? With her arms stretching high in the air, she spun in circles, over and over again. The air flowed over her delicately, the world twirling around her, and she felt free.

"It is an incredible day, isn't it?"

Draco's voice startled her. She stopped twirling; her feet touched ground. She hadn't even realized she'd been floating in the air. Turning, she faced him. He was such a stunning man and despite knowing what lay beneath, what he was capable of, her heart fluttered just to look at him. "Yes, it certainly is."

"You seem to be in a better mood."

She lowered herself all the way to the ground, slid her legs to the side and ran her hands over the soft, plush grass. "I've had some time to cool down." Her head tilted up to meet his gaze. He was so tall. Even when she stood he was much taller than she, and now, from her sitting position, he seemed like a

giant. "I guess I should apologize to you for my mood earlier."
She really hadn't been very nice to him.

"No need for that. You're entitled to your moods."

She tilted her head and looked up at him. He looked tired,
she thought. Was it possible for a demon to feel tired? She
didn't. If anything, she felt exhilarated. There was so much she
didn't know, so much she wanted to know, and he was the only
one to help her. "Take a walk with me, Draco." The look of
surprise on his face amused her.

"All right."

A faint giggle, girlish and sweet, slipped from her lips as she
stood. "Don't worry, Draco. I won't bite your head off this
time." To show a sign of peace she held her hand out to him.
Carefully, he laid his palm against hers; the electricity snapped
as always. "That is such an odd sensation," Missy said. It didn't
burn, didn't hurt much, just felt odd, sparking at their touch, as
it traveled throughout the body. And always left her feeling a
bit too warm inside.

"To say the least."

"Have you ever felt it before?" She stood and twined her
fingers between his, sealing them as one.

"Only with you."

She wasn't too sure how to respond to that. Moments of
silence passed before she spoke up again. "I'm a demon,
Draco." It was so hard to believe. It hadn't sunk in totally. She
still expected to wake from the dream. Or maybe it was a
nightmare. She wasn't quite sure yet.

His lips curved up. "So you are."

"That terrifies me," she admitted freely as they walked
along the vast property.

He stopped, turned her to face him. "It's not as bad as you
think, Missy. Once the initial shock wears off, you'll see just
how wonderful it can be."

Before Missy was able to reply, they were interrupted by
Hunter as he hurried toward them.

"Sir, there's a bit of a problem. I think you need to deal with it."

"It can wait."

"No, sir. I'm sorry, but this can't."

"It's okay. Go deal with your problem, I'm not going anywhere." Missy gave him a tiny smile as she turned to continue her walk. Maybe it was best if she wasn't near him just now. Not with all these mixed emotions swirling like a tornado inside of her.

Draco wanted to strangle Hunter with his bare hands. He had finally been able to get close to Missy, possibly get her to open up to him, and Hunter had to show up. "This better be of the utmost importance, Hunter."

"It is. Vincent has locked himself in his room. One of the maids overheard him shouting at Ian, right before she heard a gun go off." They stopped at the top of the stairs. "He's taken the maid captive."

"Is he high?"

"I don't know, sir. It's believed that he fired a weapon the other night. That must have been the sound we all heard."

Draco closed his eyes, ran his fingers through his hair, and took a deep breath. Vincent had been a thorn in his side for months now. He'd caught him high several times while on the job and hoped his last warning had been taken seriously.

Obviously not.

"Keep everyone downstairs while I deal with this." Draco marched down the hall to the last door on the right. He closed his mind to everything else and picked up Vincent's thoughts. The man was definitely high and extremely on edge. Taking a deep breath, Draco knocked. "Vincent, it's Draco. I'm coming in to talk." He inched the door open to find Vincent holding a very frightened woman by the neck. A few feet away, Ian lay on the floor in a pool of blood.

There were no signs of life.

"Stay where you are or I'll shoot her in the head."

Draco paused in the doorway, hand raised. "I just want to talk."

"I mean it. I'll shoot her."

He had no time to react when Draco vanished and reappeared behind him. In a quick move, Draco snatched the gun out of Vincent's hand and pushed him down onto his knees, arm behind his back. "Leave!" he told the maid, and it didn't take much for her to run from the room.

"Fuck!" Vincent cried out.

Draco released him with a shove and unloaded the gun. "You're high." He froze Vincent to his spot when he tried to run. "And you've murdered a man in the process. What am I to do with you, Vincent?"

"I had no choice. He came at me. He had the gun," Vince babbled.

Draco tossed the gun aside and casually walked up to Vincent. Kneeling down, he lifted his chin. "You think you can lie to me? I can read your mind, you fool!" He stood, dusting his hand off. "Now the truth."

"Ian was going to tell you I started selling," Vincent's voice quivered. "He warned me the other night. He caught me making a deal near the hedges. We wrestled and my gun went off. No one got hurt, but I took off shortly after that. Today, Ian came into my room to tell me to turn myself in or he would. I—I...wasn't thinking and grabbed my gun and...shot him," he began to sob.

"You held a gun on him only days ago and you attempted to shoot him. Am I to seriously believe today's incident was a random act?"

"No, sir."

"What am I to do with you? I now have to find some story for Ian's death." Draco walked to the patio as he thought. "Somehow work it so I'm not involved."

"I'm sorry, sir."

Draco doubted that. The only thing Vincent was sorry for

was being caught. "You need to pay for your actions."

"I know."

He turned back to the young man, his plan culminating in his mind. "Drugs are what fueled this outcome so it will be drugs that end it." He walked to Vincent, standing over him. "I believe your drug of choice is cocaine. Am I correct?"

"Yes. No! Yes," Vincent stammered.

"Cocaine it is. Let's give you the quickest high, shall we?" Stepping back, Draco produced three hypodermic needles, all filled with a cocaine suspension. They hovered mid-air over Draco's palm. "I believe injecting it will hit your system faster." He sent the first soaring toward Vincent, followed by the next, and the next. He watched as the needles struck and saw the euphoria on Vincent's face as the drug floated into his system.

His eyes went wide and Draco heard the young man's heart begin to hammer in his chest. He released his power over him and stepped back while Vincent began to convulse. The overdose of cocaine in his system would cause his heart to fail, his breathing to stop. The young man clasped his chest, and choked out a loud gasp.

Walking to him, Draco shook his head. "I warned you what your drug abuse would do." With a wave of his hand, he sent both Vincent and Ian to an alley in the city. Beside Vincent would be the weapon he'd used to end Ian's life, and three empty needles. He set the scene to seem as if Ian had been shot there, instead of in a suite several miles away. It would look like one drug-crazed man shot another before overdosing.

CHAPTER THIRTEEN

The long walk around Draco's estate did wonders for Missy's mood. She felt incredibly upbeat and refreshed. Maybe she hadn't embraced the demon she'd been forced to become, but she'd accepted it, more or less. What else could she do?

Resigned to the fact that Draco was the only person who could help her, there wasn't much else for her to do but let him teach her.

Opening the door to her suite, she was struck instantly by the pungent aroma of flowers that invaded her room. And her body quivered from head to toe.

"Do you like them?"

Missy turned to Draco, her eyes filled with wonderment. "How could one not love such a beautiful display?" Her suite had been transformed into a wonderful garden, with every flower imaginable, and she was unable to resist touching the ones closest.

"I wasn't sure what you liked, so I decided to go with a little of everything." He plucked a sprig of baby's breath and tucked it into her hair.

She touched a hand to her hair and smiled. "They're all perfect." She lifted a salmon-colored lily to her nose and drew in the aroma. The warm sensation filled her from the inside out, giving her a sense of euphoria. "It makes me feel...warm inside. Flowers have never done that to me before."

He came up behind her and ran his hands gently over her hair. Missy closed her eyes and sighed. "Flowers are a form of an aphrodisiac to demons—well, some demons at least."

Turning, the lily still in her hand, she gave Draco a puzzled look. "Really? How strange." Focusing, for a moment, on the delicate petals, she was suddenly privy to what the meaning held. Looking up at him, she wasn't sure how she felt about that. "Draco, are you trying to seduce me?"

"I wanted to show you there is beauty in being a demon."

Her body tensed. "Draco, I—"

"No, don't." He laid a finger against her soft lips. "Let me show you."

She wasn't prepared for the jolt his touch would bring her. She almost melted in his hands as his lips touched hers, but her fear rose up, and she backed away.

"I won't hurt you, Missy." He cupped her face in his hands, so gently she couldn't believe it was he who held her.

So many times before she'd felt his eyes jail hers. Now was no exception. They were dark, but not scary, filled with passion and warmth. Irresistible. "I don't know what to expect from you." She trembled.

"Only pleasure." He took her lips once more, softly, gently.

His mouth was skilled, passionate and warm. Closing her eyes, she let the sensation capture her body, resigning herself to the pleasure he gave her. He wasn't hideous now. Instead, she found he was enticing, sexual, caring and gentle, and her body reacted to him like it had never reacted before.

"Give yourself to me, Missy, and I shall show you a wealth of passion."

She tipped her head back to give his mouth room to taste. When his lips touched her skin, she felt it sizzle and her body tingled. Tiny surges of electric heat popped in every pore. When she felt his teeth, she gasped with the memory. "Draco, no!" She pushed away.

"Sssshhhh." He cupped her face in his hands and took her lips once more, quieting the panic in her throat. "Give in to me, Missy."

Her body quivered. "Don't change, please." She couldn't bear that now. What he made her feel was incredible. She wanted him and she didn't want to mar it with the sight of his demon side slipping out.

"Close your eyes and enjoy."

Her body trembled, ached, and wanted. He made her feel so alive, so needy, yet she couldn't help but fear him.

His hands skimmed over her bare arms. Shivers cascaded through her entire body. His lips took hers, first slowly, passionately, before quickening to a greedy lust. She matched him with her own greed and yielded to desire. Dipping her hands into all that thick, rich, dark hair, she gave in to the passion.

With nimble fingers, he slid the zipper at the back of her dress all the way down. Slowly, carefully, he lowered the dress from her shoulders, placing tiny kisses to the newly-bared flesh. She felt the barrier of her clothing stripped away and was helpless to his touch. Wherever flesh was exposed, his mouth followed. The further the dress slipped down, the further his lips traced. When his mouth touched her breasts, she let out a gasp and flung her head back as his mouth drew out the fire locked inside. She felt his tongue slide over her taut nipple before his mouth suckled. The gentle brush of his lips sent shock waves rebounding though every orifice of her body.

While he nibbled and teased with his mouth, his hands sought out places to arouse. Skimming over her waist, he moved to her thighs and when they slid down, over and between her legs, she let out a gasp.

He touched her, pleased her with gentle fingers caressing her folds. Sliding his mouth back up until he found hers, he drew out the passion she kept hidden deep inside.

Her eyes on his, she gasped when his clothing suddenly disappeared. The shock of his nudity rocked her. She hadn't known what to expect, but not that, not that he would look and feel so much like a man, so incredibly human. Right now that was all he was, and she had trouble denying how much she wanted him. "Take me, Draco."

"We have time." His lips whispered against hers and she shuddered. Slowly, he touched every part of her body with his hands, his lips, and tongue.

His hands skimmed over her nude body as he walked around her. Pushing her hair away, he leaned in and kissed the soft, sensitive part of her neck just below her ear. She trembled. His hands slid over her while his mouth traced the outline of her back, the curve of her spine, the dip in her waist. With his mouth and hands working her into a frenzy, he eased around until they were face to face, mouth to mouth, body to body. "Now," he whispered against her mouth as his tongue teased hers.

Now, dear God, now! She felt crazy with need, desperate to have, to touch, to feel. He was tormenting her with his touch, with his lips. Her entire body ached with a pain she'd never felt before. If he didn't ease it now, she would scream. "Now!"

He took her lips to his and devoured her mouth as their bodies lifted from the ground. Slowly they moved, floating weightlessly, turning to give him easier access. "Look at me, Missy." Her lashes fluttered open. "Look at me."

She let out a gasp at what she saw. His eyes were blood red, and staring at her with such an intense passion it left her breathless. She felt the surge of sharp heat as he entered her. He was like no man she had even known before. He was large, spreading her as he pressed deeper inside. With the pain came the pleasure, so much incredible pleasure. His eyes forgotten, her desires controlling, she opened and gave, and in return, she took.

Together they floated above the ground, their bodies linked as one. While he held her, kissed her, tormenting her with his hands, he moved inside of her with perfect rhythm.

He pressed deep inside of her, making her body come alive

in ways she never thought possible. His mouth on her breasts drew out so much passion it nearly overwhelmed her. She growled as her body was inundated with one shuddering orgasm after another. He let out a deep growl that sunk right to the pit of her core. She felt him jerk inside her as his orgasm peaked. It seemed to last forever, his hot seed spilling into her. Tipping her head back, she howled while her body twitched and quivered.

Their love produced a storm that shook the foundations of Missy's world.

CHAPTER FOURTEEN

Missy had never felt so alive before, so fulfilled, and she hadn't realized how much she'd craved love until now. She'd just made love to a demon and she wasn't the slightest bit repulsed or frightened. Had she known he could make her feel so alive, she would have given in to him long ago. Despite feeling a little sore, she reveled in the gloriousness her body felt.

Draco rolled over and traced his fingers over her forehead, brushing the hair from her face. "I can never read your thoughts. Everyone else's thoughts are jumping out at me, yet yours elude me. I wish I knew why. Can you read mine?"

She didn't feel the slightest bit awkward lying naked beside him now. If anything, she felt at ease. "I don't know. I haven't tried. Not sure I want to, though."

His finger trailed over her face, along her jaw, and down to her full soft lips. "Give it a try. I'm curious. It's baffling to me that I can't read yours."

His finger was managing to arouse her even though they'd just finished taking each other. Open, her mind and body relaxing, his thoughts slipped into her mind. He was happy, aroused as much as she was and there, beneath those emotions, she sensed his confusion.

Can you read my thoughts? he asked her, inside her mind.

"Yes," she responded. "Odd that you can't read mine."

"Very."

She closed her eyes and let his fingers tease her skin. He brought out so many emotions, feelings she never knew existed before. Maybe there was more to this demon stuff than she thought. If everything felt so incredible, being a demon couldn't be half bad. "Am I still human?"

"Partially. You are half human and half demon."

She trailed her finger along his arm. It was muscular, but not overly bulky. His skin felt no different from hers, yet she knew the other side of him. "Are you? Part human?"

He laid his hand over hers. "I am full-blood demon."

"Do you heal quickly?"

"Within seconds."

"Mine takes a little longer than that. When I was shot in the shoulder, it took a while to heal over. Not nearly as long as it did before I became a demon, though."

Draco bolted up, grabbing hold of her. "You were shot? When?"

She pulled away. The worry she saw in his face was a bit unsettling. "That night you found me outside, the night I was trying to leave. I'm fine, Draco, I healed. Troy helped me—"

His hands stopped stroking her face and his eyes narrowed. "What do you mean, Troy helped you?"

"He explained everything to me. He made me realize I'd been shot and told me I was a demon, like you." She didn't like that look in Draco's eyes, a dangerous warning look.

"Troy knew of you?" The fury lighting his eyes made her tense.

"Yes." His hands dug into her shoulders and it took a great deal of effort to pry them loose. She sat holding them, not sure what he would do if she let them go.

"What else did he do with you?" He spoke through gritted teeth, his voice low. He was definitely pissed, and she wasn't impressed by it.

"Nothing." Oh, she really didn't like that look now. His eyes grew even darker, more intense.

He let out a low growl, much like a tiger readying to attack. "Did he claim your body?"

"Claim? What are you talking about?"

"Did he have sex with you?" he shouted, and it made her jump.

It took her off guard, a momentary lapse, and for a moment, she thought she was in her home and Ronald was the one yelling at her once again. Suddenly, the flecks of red lashing out from Draco's eyes drew her back. "What? No!" She barely got the last word out when he bolted from the bed.

He waved his hand and instantly was dressed in a pair of navy pants. "He took what was mine." He stormed into her sitting room and with a sweep of his hand, the flowers disappeared.

"Draco, wait!" Wrapping the blanket around her body, she went after him. She really didn't like his temper, or the sound he made deep in his throat. It reminded her a great deal of an animal about to strike. "Draco—" He cut her off with a wave of his hand and Troy stood before them. "Draco, stop!" she pleaded as she rushed to his side. She had a sickening feeling she knew what would happen next.

Troy's eyes widened and the look of shock was clear on his face.

Draco narrowed his eyes at the young man and pulled his arm free from Missy's grasp. "What happens to people who disobey me, Troy?"

Troy swallowed loudly. "They're punished."

"Draco, don't." She grabbed his arm but he shook her off. She wouldn't let him do this.

"You deceived me, hid her from me and took what was mine. I won't tolerate it." He lifted a fiery hand and sent a ball of heat soaring at Troy.

The direct hit sent Troy flying like he was no more than a child's toy, in the air, until his body hit the wall with a thud.

"Draco, stop it now!" Missy went to Troy and was abruptly stopped and lifted off her feet. She was carried through the air only to land harshly on the sofa-chair. More furious than shocked, she fought to break free, and was unable to. "Draco!" she screamed at him while she struggled to break his hold.

Ignoring her, Draco focused on Troy. He lifted the smaller man off his feet and sent him crashing into another wall several feet away.

Missy's fury erupted like a long-stilled volcano. She snapped Draco's control like a twig. Breaking free, she aimed hot fury directly at Draco. He gasped as his body lunged back and was pinned against the wall.

Rising from the chair, she hurried over to Troy, all the while still pinning Draco to the wall with no effort at all. "I will not permit this type of behavior," she spat at Draco while she checked for a pulse. Like a flash, the vision came to her and made her gasp. She could see it, see all the way inside of Troy, and she saw the damage Draco had done.

It took her a moment to grasp what she saw, another to try to deal with it. Closing her eyes, she took a deep breath. She saw the broken bones, bruises, and blood, so much blood. She needed to get hold of herself before moving on.

"Missy, release me now!" he ordered in a loud booming voice.

Ignoring Draco, Missy ran her hands over the wounds. "Heal." When Troy's eyes opened and he drew in a deep breath, she stood. "Go, Troy. Now."

He gripped the wall while he got to his feet. "Thank you."

She tipped her head, waving him away. Turning to Draco, she could feel his powers fighting hers, but she held strong.

"Release me, Missy. Immediately!" he demanded once more, his eyes blazing.

She narrowed her eyes, wiped a hand over her mouth, before releasing him. She didn't feel the slightest bit winded or drained, and how she had managed to do what she did was unfathomable to her. Yet she had.

"You are never to do that again," he warned her as he rolled his shoulders.

"*I* do as *I* please," she spat back at him venomously. "I did not have sex with Troy, and even if I had, it is no business of yours."

His dark eyes narrowed in on her. "He knew I was searching for you. His mistake was failing to inform me that you had been found. I do not tolerate insubordination."

"For that you would kill him?"

"Yes."

She stared at him in disbelief. "So you would kill anyone who disobeys you?" He was cold. The man she'd made love to wasn't the man she saw before her now. There were so many sides to him. Which one was the true Draco? She had a feeling the one she saw before her now was the one.

"He didn't just disobey me. He deliberately hid you from me and lied to me."

"He did nothing of the sort. I asked him not to tell you until I was ready. It's no wonder the staff walks on eggshells around you. Tell me, Draco, how many have you disposed of for minor infractions?" she asked him in a low, dry tone with just a hint of ridicule.

"My staff respects me."

Her laughter rippled through the room. "Respect? Oh no, Draco, they fear you. I pity you, Draco." Shaking her head, she turned from him.

"You pity me?" He grabbed her arm and spun her to face him. "I have everything I could possibly want at my disposal. Whatever I want, I take."

She had no doubt about that. "You have nothing without love and respect, Draco, and that has to be earned," she stated calmly as her eyes focused her pity on him.

His hands balled into fists at his sides. "I am in authority here. I have loyal employees that have been around for years."

"You have minions who fear you, Draco, oblige you because they fear you. They don't dare cross you for fear it will cost them their lives. Tell me, when are their birthdays? Do they have families? Do you know them? Have you ever sat down to a meal with any of them?" She saw the answer in his eyes as he lowered them. "What a lonely life you must lead."

His gaze lifted to hers. "My lonely days are over now that I have you."

"You don't have me, Draco. I belong to no one but myself. I am no man's tool. Not now, not ever again." This time, she was in control.

He clenched, unclenched his jaw. "You are mine, Missy. Without me, you can't survive."

"With an ego that size, I'm surprised you can keep your swollen head so high." She waved her hand at him, dismissing him absently. What once terrified her now saddened her. What a sad man, what a sad life he must lead. She did pity him. He had no idea what living really was. "Go, Draco. I can't look at you right now." He stepped forward, but she held her hand up, stopping him.

"I will leave you, for now, but I will not stay away from you." He vanished at the last of his words.

Missy blew out a breath as she dropped down on the sofa. Her entire body quivered, but not of fear. No more fear. She had just gone toe-to-toe with a demon much older and stronger than she was, yet she overpowered him. How on earth she'd accomplished that was beyond her. The thrill she felt with that knowledge was exhilarating. She had just controlled a demon, had looked inside a man's body and healed him with only a thought. This wasn't like the woman she'd been. Oh no, she was completely different now.

Dear God, what the hell had she become?

CHAPTER FIFTEEN

Draco sat in his office, his fingers drumming so loudly on his desk, the sound echoed in the stillness of the room. He was furious.

"Sir, is everything all right?" Hunter asked, stepping quietly into the office.

"No, everything is not all right." His fingers left tiny grooves in the wood as they drummed.

"Is there a problem?"

"Yes, and her name is Missy Green."

"Oh."

"She happens to be quite powerful." Hell, that was a tame word for what she held inside of her. How she was so strong was beyond him.

"Is she, sir?"

Draco waved his hand and had a chair sliding out for Hunter. "Sit, Hunter. Your stiffness is only making me feel worse."

Hunter took a seat and waited for Draco to speak.

"She pinned me." He dug at a splinter in his desk. Humiliation had him keeping his eyes to the desk. "With no more than a casual look, she pinned me to the wall and held me there."

"Impossible, sir!"

"I assure you it is quite possible and she did." At this rate, he'd have the desk in splinters. Waving his hand, he held a cigarette, not that he really wanted it, but it occupied his hands. "I've never felt strength like hers before. It was magnificent, ferocious. She used it as if she'd been born to it and used it her entire life." He'd encountered several who dared to challenge him, but he'd always been the strongest, until now. Her power definitely outmatched his.

Hunter sat forward, genuinely concerned. "You've been around much longer and your powers are far more superior."

Draco smiled. "Hunter, you please me." So what if he needed his ego stroked? Was that such a bad thing? He scowled to himself, remembering the hurtful words Missy had said about his ego. "Tell me something, Hunter. Do you respect me?"

"Of course, sir."

Draco stared at him a moment as he drew on his cigarette. The answer came out so quickly he wasn't sure if it was instinct or if he really meant it. So he looked into his mind. "Do you love me?"

"Unconditionally, sir. I would give my life for yours."

He knew one thing for sure, Hunter was sincere. "Take the rest of the day off, Hunter." Draco felt warm from the thoughts, the sincerity of Hunter's feelings. It touched him deeply to feel so much admiration from his dear friend. "You deserve it."

Obviously stunned, Hunter gaped before speaking. "Uh, beg pardon, sir?"

"You heard me. Take the rest of the day off. Relax. Do something for yourself."

"Thank you, sir." Hunter stood and gave his jacket a tug, before turning to leave.

Draco's gaze followed Hunter as he left. Was he that hard of a man? Apparently he was. Odd, how suddenly that would bother him. Drawing on his cigarette, he sighed.

Maybe it was time for a change. But before that happened,

he needed more answers. Snapping his fingers, Troy sat in the very chair Hunter just vacated.

The look of both shock and fear was clear on Troy's face. "Draco, let me—"

Draco lifted one hand and silenced Troy. "Let me begin." He was hard, but he had been hurt and angry. He crushed out his cigarette and did something he never felt a need to do before. "I must apologize for my rage earlier, but I'm sure you can understand my anger."

"Yes, sir. I can understand your anger."

He read the young man before him as clearly as if Troy's inner thoughts were written on his face. Troy was afraid of Draco, and before Missy's stinging comments, he would have reveled in that. But not now. Oh, truth was a hard thing to deal with. "So, you found her? Why is it you felt you didn't need to inform me that you had found her?"

"She asked me not to, and...looking back on it now, I should have just gone to you and told you."

"Yes, you should have. I expect loyalty from my employees. I will stand nothing less."

"Yes, sir." Troy lowered his head.

Draco could read every thought inside the boy's mind, including his deigns to seduce Missy. Draco was not impressed. "You'd hoped to bed her."

Troy's head whipped up, his eyes wide. "No, sir!"

"Careful with your thoughts, boy. You might not like my reaction," Draco warned calmly.

Troy bit his lip. "I forgot. Sorry."

Draco leaned in very close, placing his wide hands palm-down on his desk. "She's mine. Remember that."

"Yes, sir."

"You won't touch what is mine. Is that understood, Troy?"

"Yes, sir." Troy trembled at the look in Draco's eyes and the low tone his voice had taken on.

"I am nobody's property, Draco." Missy stepped into the room. "Go away, Troy." She waved her hand and he disappeared. "I am a strong, independent, free-thinking woman and you need to remember that."

"I never said otherwise."

She continued to stare at him. "I am not one of your minions. I will not bow at your feet or cower to you."

"I never asked you to."

"I was dominated by one man already, Draco. I won't make that mistake twice."

"I have no intention of dominating you." He just sat back, smoked his cigarette and let her roll.

"I am not yours, Draco. Remember that."

His eyes narrowed as he stared at her. "It was I that drew out the creature you are now. You should remember that." He stood, tapped out his cigarette.

Her eyes narrowed in on his, challenging him. "I wouldn't feel pride in that, Draco. I have yet to decide if that suits me or not."

"Whether you like it or not, Missy, you are what you are. It would go a lot easier if you just accepted it."

"I've accepted it. What choice do I have? That doesn't mean I have to like what happened to me."

Walking around the desk, he came up beside her. "So be it, but while you're deciding whether you like it or not, I will need to teach you how to control it."

"I can control it." She waved her hand and had the lights going off. One more wave and they came on again. "See? A piece of cake."

Good grief, she was magnificent in every way. "There is more to it than just that."

"There are things I draw the line at, Draco. I refuse to eat people."

He nearly snickered at the way she said that. "I suspected as much, and for the record, I don't eat people either. But there will come a time, Missy, when the urge to kill, to feed, will overcome you. I need to teach you how to suppress it."

She stepped away. "You will teach me to suppress it?" She

let out a tiny mocking laugh. "You would teach me? You didn't suppress it when you attacked Jennifer."

"I was left with no other choice." And he didn't much care for her constantly throwing that in his face.

She let out a snort of a laugh. "No choice. You could have let her walk away."

"No, I couldn't."

She stared at him, her face cold. "Tell me, Draco, why you couldn't just walk away from her?"

He tucked his hands in his pockets to keep them from reaching out to her, when he knew she would only pull away. "She was distraught."

"Distraught. I can't imagine why." She tapped her head lightly. "Maybe it was the fact that she woke up with a demon lurking over her." Her voice was dry and cold and aimed directly at him.

He bit back his attitude and reminded himself to stay calm. "The drug didn't hold." He had yet to figure out why.

"Apparently. So instead of trying to calm her down you killed her."

"I wasn't able to calm her down. The mind isn't so easily controlled when a person is hysterical," he explained, not entirely sure she was really grasping anything he was saying. "She'd gone mad, she was tearing at her own flesh."

Missy stared at him, uncomprehending.

"Do you remember how you could see inside Troy?" Draco began haltingly. "I could see her. Jennifer. Her mind was...damaged. Some humans are so fragile. I had no choice but to end her life."

"I will never be like you, Draco." She turned away from him. "Never."

"You are like me, Missy. You won't ever be normal again." He turned her to face him. "You will notice as time moves on, more and more of you will be like me." He saw the pain hit her eyes and felt it ricochet inside of him. "It's not so bad. You won't need regular sleep, you won't need to worry about regularly scheduled meals. You'll eat only when you are hungry. You won't feel any of the regular ailments that humans do, and you won't age. I should think all of those would make you feel better."

"Well, it doesn't."

"Missy—"

"No, don't. Just let me be."

He reached out for her, but she vanished before he could touch her. Rubbing a hand over his face, he let out a rush of air. How could he make her understand? There were things she needed to know, things that were vital she know, but he sensed he would only be talking to a brick wall if he tried to explain them to her. He hadn't wanted to kill that young woman; doing so had taken a lot out of him. The ache it left inside didn't seem to want to leave him this time.

Some might say Draco felt guilt at killing an innocent victim. Draco chose to call it rational thought. Taking a life was not an easy task. Innocent people weren't meant to die, only vile human beings. When he'd murdered, so many decades ago, they'd been lowlifes, murderers themselves. Never had he taken the life of an innocent.

Until now. Until Jennifer.

Sighing, he rested a hip on his desk. Missy needed to know all there was to being demon, the good and the bad. If only he felt she wanted to learn.

CHAPTER SIXTEEN

The house was entirely too empty now that Draco had sent the Starr Gazers on a trip eastward. How could a person live here with all this silence? Then again, Draco wasn't a normal person, and now, neither was she.

Missy let out a heavy sigh. What was she to do from here?

She couldn't go home, not to her family. There was no way she would be able to live near them day after day, month after month, without explaining why she didn't sleep like they did, or eat the kinds of foods they did. Never mind the fact that she wouldn't ever get sick or injured, let alone age. It would be impossible to live near them and continually lie to them. Therefore, she could never go home again. That hurt so much it nearly crippled her.

She stepped outside and walked toward the gardens. The sun was rising, another day over, one more beginning. Where would she go from here? She couldn't lead a normal life. Staying in one place too long was unthinkable. And what if she became injured, how would she explain the lack of blood? The human body didn't heal itself in a matter of seconds.

Would she ever be able to have a relationship with a man again? Not without telling him what she really was. She had a life of loneliness ahead of her.

No lovers, no husband, no children. What was the point? Was that why Draco secluded himself? Here, he was safe to do as he pleased, so far away from civilization. She let out a restless sigh and dropped down on the grass.

She sensed Draco as he came up behind her and his thoughts rang out to her as clearly as if he'd spoken them aloud. *She looks so sad. I wish I could read her mind and know what she is feeling.*

"I'm blue, Draco, and don't you know it's impolite to spy on a person?" She plucked at the grass, a little miffed. All she wanted was to be alone, to wallow, and now here he was, invading her mind. It was bothersome to have others' thoughts in her mind. At times it was nearly enough to drive her over the edge. She didn't like it one bit.

"I wasn't spying. I was merely wandering my own grounds. I tend to do that when I'm restless." He sat down on the grass beside her. "I'm not sure I like you reading my mind." He plucked a blade of grass and had it blooming into a beautiful purple bell.

"I *know* I don't like reading it, but what can I do?" She took the tiny flower and produced a dozen. Laying them on the grass, she had them rooting in the ground.

"I could teach you to block them out."

"I would appreciate that." It would be nice to block out his thoughts. The emotions he felt for her were a bit too much to handle. She just wasn't ready to feel what he felt. She had given herself completely to a man before, and it nearly cost her life.

"I wasn't sure you would speak to me after our last encounter."

She shrugged one shoulder. "I've mostly gotten over that."

"So, what is it that has you so blue?"

"Life. My endless lonely life."

"Ah." He took hold of her hand and toyed with her fingers. "You feel lonely."

"I feel hopeless." She pulled her hand free. "I'll never have any normalcy in my life, no friends, no family, no boyfriends, no husband, no children." She sighed and crushed one of the blooms in her hand.

He waved his hand and had it coming back to life. "You will have me."

Her shoulders dropped as she lifted her eyes to his. "No offense, Draco, but that just doesn't cut it." She regretted her words instantly when she saw the hurt blossom over his face. "That was rude of me. I'm sorry."

"Let me show you the wonders of your powers." He got to his feet and held out his hand for her.

"Draco, I'm really not in the mood to be taught right now." She was comfortable in her self-pity.

He took her hand and pulled her to her feet. "What better time to lift your spirits than when they are down?" Lifting her hand to his lips, he placed a gentle kiss to her knuckles. "Now, do as I say." She tilted her head and shot him a nasty look. "I'm not ordering you, Missy. It was a request."

"It sure sounded like an order to me." And she wished he would stop thinking already. Hearing his thoughts: how beautiful she was, how much he enjoyed her touch; was a bit overwhelming.

"Sorry. I should have said it more like this." He pulled her against him and her eyes widened in surprise. "Close your eyes and try to follow my words."

Relenting, Missy closed her eyes, and drew in a deep breath. She loved the cologne he always wore. It wasn't strong and overpowering. It was more like a gentle breeze caressing her senses.

"Good. Now, let your body go. Relax every muscle. Visualize them. Stroke them until they are lax." His hands rested gently on her arms.

She laughed. "How am I supposed to do that?"

"Relax and breathe."

Taking another deep breath, she did her best to relax. It was no easy task. Not when she felt so wound-up and miserable.

"Let yourself go."

Missy focused on the tension in her muscles. In no time, she could feel it slip away.

"Good. Now, go deep inside your mind. Close off everything else but my voice. Imagine being completely invisible. No one but you and I can see you, know that you are there."

"Wow, I feel so...light." It was as if her body were made of air, and what an interesting sensation that was.

She's good, very good, for a beginner.

"Why, thank you." Opening her eyes, she grinned back at him.

He shook his head, a smile easing its way to his lips. "I must figure out how to block myself from you before you read something I have no intention for you to know."

"Secrets, Draco," she tapped a finger to his lips. "Never stay buried for long."

"I believe you are right." His smile drew out lines to add more charm to an already handsome face. Leaning in, he brushed his lips against hers and just lingered for a few moments before releasing her. "I still need to figure out why I have such an incredible urge to taste and touch your lips with mine."

She angled her head. "You've never kissed someone before?" How was that possible when he seemed so skilled at it, so perfect?

"Of course I have, but only to appease them." He touched her lips once more. "With you, it seems I want to have them, need to have them. All the time."

The emotions she felt from him nearly overwhelmed her. She didn't know how to handle it all, so she chose to try to ignore it. "Why am I invisible?"

"I want to take you soaring." He slid his hand down her arm to join hands, and slowly brought it to his chest. "Now, we fly." While his eyes stayed locked to hers, he took them up, way up, over the clouds, and into the calm blue sky.

She gasped, clinging to him, afraid she would fall. "Don't drop me."

He laughed and tightened his arms around her. "I won't let you go. I will never let you go. Hold on if you like, but trust me, you are as light as air." He released her momentarily. "See, you too can float."

"Draco, don't!" She dove at him, clinging for dear life. They were so high up. Everything below looked so small. Houses looked like toys on a child's bedroom floor. The people moving about looked like ants and the vehicles resembled miniature cars on a racetrack. It terrified her.

"All right, I'll hold you." Smiling, he pulled her closer. "But you won't fall, not until you're ready to let yourself down."

They soared over cities, over towns and villages, and beyond. Once she overcame her fear of heights, she began to loosen up and enjoy the ride. It was the most incredible feeling, to be so high and so free. Missy never wanted to come down ever again. It all seemed so wonderful, so unreal, yet so real. She felt incredible and her earlier blue mood was long forgotten.

Spotting a young man about to be run down by a car, she pulled him out of harm's way using the power of her mind.

"You shouldn't do that," Draco admonished.

She turned to Draco, her face beaming with pride. It was an incredible feeling, having saved someone from what could very well have led to death. "Do what, save a person's life?"

"Each human has his time. You shouldn't alter reality or their destinies." He stroked her hair as she looked at him in confusion.

He had morals. That truly surprised her. "What good are my powers if I can't help someone in need?"

He turned her to face him and held her by the shoulders as they hovered high in the clouds. "There is a natural order of life. Souls are created, nurtured, they live and die. By altering even a small part, you alter reality and their destiny and possibility those of others as well."

She pushed a cloud away as it drifted into her view, not really comprehending the fact that she floated on her own now, without Draco holding her. "So I can't prevent someone from dying, but it's okay to heal someone?" She was more than a little confused.

He took her hands in his and played with her fingers while his gaze stayed steady on hers. "If that person was hurt by you, it's okay to heal them."

"I healed Troy even though it wasn't me that injured him. Was that wrong?"

"Troy isn't human. Demons live by different rules. Their souls are already tarnished and at any given time can be called back down to Hell."

"Will that happen to me now?" She didn't want to go to Hell.

He stroked her face with such loving that it took her breath away. "I would never let that happen. I would give my soul for yours rather than let you go to Hell."

She was stunned by the emotion not only in his voice, but in his mind as well. He meant every word he said. "You surprise me, Draco. I thought you were a cold-hearted bastard who stole souls and caused people nothing but pain."

The hurt she saw on his face made her regret her words.

"Oh, Missy, it is no wonder you were so reluctant to be near me." He cupped her face in his hands and kissed her gently. "There are many kinds of demons. Not all are evil. True, some walk the earth with the sole purpose of killing and causing pain, but I assure you, I am not one of them, not anymore. I did my time."

"Time doing what?"

"Hundreds of years ago I was sent here, to earth, to collect souls for Satan. It was the only way I was allowed to leave Hell. What I did in my past is not something I care to discuss. It was a different time. I was a different person."

She remembered Troy telling her something about that. "But you do still take lives." She thought of Jennifer and the way he had ended her life. Would she ever be able to look at him and not see what he'd done to a poor frightened young girl?

He stroked her cheek with his hand. "I have, I do, but only when necessary. You're thinking of Jennifer. No, I can't read your mind, but it's not hard to guess where that statement came from. I've weaned myself off of human blood. Tasting hers was like ambrosia and it's taken me time to quell the need to drink more human blood. There are times when the need to feast on flesh and blood is so overwhelming, you can't go on without it. Blood-lust is a powerful drug."

She could easily go on without it. It was time to change the subject. "I could really get used to this, floating on clouds." She gave the fluffy white cloud beside her a pat and a dusting of white mist floated around her. "I wonder, is this one cloud nine?" she giggled as she looked up at Draco.

"You can't claim to be on cloud nine until you've made love on one." He took her hand in his, raised it to his lips, and nibbled.

Her body vibrated from his simple touch. "We couldn't." But oh, how she wanted him.

He pulled her closer, her breath heavy. "We can." He undid the first of the many buttons on her dress.

"But someone could see us." She looked around and realized how silly that was. "Well, you know what I mean."

He smiled as he slid the dress from her shoulders. "No one can see us." He traced tiny kisses along her neck and her body quivered.

"I can't." His tongue dipped down to slip under the lace of her bra and she gasped. "Oh, Draco."

Opening her dress completely, he slid his hands over her body. The garment vanished, leaving her bare but for her bra and panties. While his mouth aroused her, his hands removed the last remaining items of clothing. She couldn't believe what she was allowing, what she was doing. The air rushed over her bare skin, creating a plethora of sensations that left her breathless. She was floating on a cloud while he worked her body into a frenzy. That alone filled her with excitement. His mouth worked its way further down, sliding softly along her breasts, nibbling as he moved to her belly. She looked down as he buried his face between her legs.

He had been correct, floating on a cloud held much more meaning to her now. His mouth devoured, his tongue teased and his teeth scraped, creating waves of pleasure, which bounced around inside her. Her body quivered with each touch. Ronald had never made her feel this way, and she found she wanted to experience it—experience Draco—dozens of times over.

He brought his mouth back to hers, letting her taste the nature of her own juices as he slowly pressed inside. Again the sharp sting of desire ran through her as he entered and filled her so completely. With her head tilted back, her back arched, she welcomed him deep, where the warmth longed to be touched.

Together they rolled over clouds and air. Dust from the white cumulus clouds covered them, wrapping them in their silky smooth texture as their bodies soared above the ground and beyond passion.

When she felt the heat of her orgasm pulsate inside of her, she arched her back, dug her nails into his arms, and screamed out as her body convulsed.

She truly was on cloud nine.

CHAPTER SEVENTEEN

"**W**e really need to start out in a bed some time," she giggled girlishly as they set down inside his room. She felt incredible. No words could describe how free and alive she felt at that very moment.

"Beds are for the ordinary." He grinned as he pulled her into his arms. "We are anything but."

She wrapped her arms around his neck, enjoying the intimacy of the moment. "That's true, but still."

"You didn't enjoy being on cloud nine?" He stroked the hair from her face, his fingers gentle as they caressed her skin.

"Oh, I enjoyed it very much. But cuddling in bed after lovemaking is so relaxing." She sent them to his bed without any effort whatsoever.

"Your abilities astound me." He tucked her under his arm, her head resting on his shoulder. *Oh, this is nice. I rather like cuddling.*

"Told you." She grinned up at him, his thoughts as clear to her as if he'd spoken them aloud. "You have the same abilities as me. What's so astounding about mine?" Resting her head on his shoulder once more, she trailed a finely pointed nail along his chest and felt him quiver. Now that was a nice feeling.

"The fact that you're so strong after being a demon for only a short period is what is so astounding."

"Are you still upset because I pinned you?"

"No one has ever overpowered me." He kissed her head. "Before you, that is."

She lifted her head and looked up at him with confusion. "No one?"

"No." He kissed her nose. "And don't let that go to that pretty head of yours." He slid his hand over her face and smiled.

"Oh, I won't." She had the advantage here, and wasn't that wonderful?

Grabbing hold of her by the waist, he flipped her in one quick motion, making her gasp. The shock gave way to pleasure and she couldn't stop from giggling.

"I love it when you laugh." He held her to the mattress and her pulse raced.

She looked up into his dark eyes. Those eyes had felt like a jail to her once; now as he looked down at her, she saw only passion. "Thank you for lightening my mood."

"Anytime."

In a flash she flipped him on his back and pinned his hands over his head.

"You are deriving too much pleasure from overpowering me."

Smiling, she lowered down with the illusion of kissing him. "Yes, I am." She bit his bottom lip instead. "And I love it." Still pinning him, she kissed him while he scowled at her inside his mind. "Don't worry, Draco, I won't tell anyone I'm stronger than you. I wouldn't want to bruise your ego." She rested her head back on his chest and sighed. She did things with him she never would have dared to do with Ronald. But thinking of the man she'd run from right after making love to another man was a horrible thought. Ronald was her past. She needed to keep him there.

He gave her hip a pinch and smiled when she squealed. "You're too kind." Pulling her closer, he leaned his cheek on her head. "We need to find out why you are so powerful."

She nuzzled into his chest and sighed. "Why?" This was the only place she wanted to be right now. Beyond this was nothing: no worries, no fear, no heartache.

"I'm curious."

"Curious, huh? Or maybe you want to match it," she spoke lazily.

Lifting her face by the chin, he looked at her with an earnest expression. "No, I'm simply curious."

She smiled at him, nipped at his lips before resting her head back on his chest. He could believe that if he liked, but she could read his mind. "Your mouth says one thing, Draco, but your mind says another."

"I must find a way to block my thoughts. You were adopted," he informed her, shifting the subject.

"Yes." Where he was going with this question, Missy wasn't too sure.

"Your birth mother's name was Michelle Dawson."

She lifted her head again and looked up at him quizzically. "You really were thorough." Why had she expected anything different from him?

He kissed her nose and smiled. "You intrigued me. I wanted to know all there was to know about you."

She supposed that should have upset her, but somehow it didn't. "What does my being adopted have to do with anything?"

"It doesn't." He pressed her head back down on his chest. "Only that your mother was human."

"That means my father was a demon."

"Yes." *And you'll never know him if I have anything to do with it.*

"Your thoughts are crowding me, Draco. Ease up." She took a breath as she sat up. "Do you know my father?" The blankets slid from her body. She didn't bother to cover up. She was too dazed by his thoughts.

Damn my thoughts. Maybe I can distract her away from

this subject—

She scowled at him as she lifted the blankets over her breasts. "Damn your thoughts later. Who is my father and why don't you want me to meet him?"

He sat up and rested against the wooden headboard. "I really must learn to curb my thoughts."

"Draco."

"Fine. I knew him."

"Tell me about him."

"Why?"

She let out a huff. "Because he's my father. I'm curious about the man—demon—that created me." She hadn't wanted to know before, but now the information seemed vital.

With a wave of his hand, he held a cigarette. He drew in long and hard before responding. "All right. His name was Pythos and he was a nasty SOB who enjoyed inflicting pain on others. It's a rule that no demon is allowed to mate with a human. The punishment is a fierce one. Your father broke that rule and was punished for it."

"What's the big deal about mating with a human?"

He drew in slowly before blowing the smoke up in the air. "Satan doesn't have control over those born half-demon."

Oddly, she felt reassured by that. "What was the punishment?"

He cleared his throat, drew on his cigarette. "You don't need to know that," he stated after blowing a ring of smoke overhead.

She grabbed his cigarette and made it vanish. "Yes I do. Tell me."

Lifting his brow, he continued. "Fine. He was called back to Hell, hung by his toes, his skin flayed from his bones."

His words sunk deep into her, curling in her stomach like a fierce tornado. She swallowed. "That's absolutely horrible."

"He wasn't a very nice man and broke the prime rule."

"Still...will that happen to you? I'm part human? I don't want that to happen to you."

He silenced her with a soft kiss. "You're also part demon."

Yes she was, and it made her wonder. Was she like her father, in any way? "Was he stronger than you?"

He let out a loud hardy laugh. "Hardly." *Pythos was half the man I am.*

She narrowed her eyes on him. "Your ego's showing." Draco sure was full of himself. "If you're so much more powerful and superior, why am I stronger than you?" she asked with a cocky grin.

"Your reading my mind is pissing me off."

"Imagine how your employees must feel when you probe theirs."

He scowled at her. "I tune them out for the most part. I don't delve into their privacy."

"Oh, now you're pouting." She poked at his lip and grinned.

He pushed her hand away. "I am not."

"Pouty baby," she teased him.

"Stop it."

"Make me," she challenged, openly, daringly.

His eyes slanted and grew very dark, and they matched the thoughts he had running through his mind.

"You wouldn't?" She backed away, not in fear, but out of distrust. His mind had turned very dirty.

"You dare challenge me?" He reached out for her but she slipped just out of his reach.

His thoughts were very clear. He would tie her to the bed and tickle her until she gave in. She would be defenseless. He would have her and there would be nothing she could do about it.

"Draco, be nice." She held her hands up to block him, holding him to his spot. Sometimes reading a mind came in handy. At least she would be prepared. But when the room filled with flowers, she learned pinning a demon did little to stop him when he wanted something badly enough. "Oh, that's dirty." The fragrant aroma teased her senses and aroused her body.

"Yes, it is." Her powers gave. Draco attacked and pinned her to the bed.

With her body too fired up to defend herself, she actually feared what he might do next. She hated being tickled. "Draco, don't. Please," she panted as his body pressed against hers.

"Begging won't stop me. When I want something, I get it." He yanked her arms above her head, wrapping his hand around both her wrists while the other lowered to her side. "And I want to see you suffer."

"No, stop. Don't even think about it." But it was a futile attempt. His hand touched her side and he began his torture. "Draco...stop it," she panted between giggles, writhing to get away from his torment.

"I'm sorry. I can't oblige you that. Ask me later." He tickled some more.

Pulling her hands free, she flipped him over, pinning him to the bed. She was stronger than he was and he needed to remember that. She devoured his lips while her hands worked over him with such fervor it had him gasping. With her tongue probing his mouth, she lowered down onto him and took him in with one swift drive.

She felt insane with control. Pulling her mouth free of his, she sat up and arched her back while he pushed deep inside of her. His hands found her breasts and squeezed while she took them on a ride beyond ecstasy, beyond reasoning, beyond fulfillment. She rode him like a wild beast, her body rocking over his. She felt him deep inside, a steel-iron rod probing as it drew out the release. They exploded in one hard shudder that had them both collapsing.

Laughing and panting, she fell onto the bed. "That will teach you to play dirty."

"Oh, Missy, how foolish of you to think that would discourage me." He rolled over and climbed on top of her, holding her hands above her head.

He had the most wicked look in his eyes, and her body heated to it instantly. "Did I say I was trying to discourage you?"

Laughing, he brought his lips to hers. "I stand corrected." He took her back over the edge.

Chapter Eighteen

Three hours in bed satisfying her most carnal desires didn't exhaust Missy. Instead, she felt high, energetic, alive. And with all that pent-up energy, her mind worked overtime. Draco had told her about her father, and from the sounds of it, he wasn't a very nice man. It made her think and wonder about her mother. She had been human. How did she die? What had she been like? With her adoptive mother gone, and not wanting to ask her father about the details, Missy figured she would never find out about the woman who gave birth to her.

Stepping out of the shower, her hair still damp, she posed her question to Draco while he dressed. "How did you get the information on me?"

He drew up the zipper on his pants as he responded. "I asked Hunter to do the research."

"Okay, but how did he get it?"

Glancing in the mirror, Draco smoothed out his damp hair. "He went to the hall of records and retrieved your folder."

"Did he get any information on my mother?" She opened her closet and was stunned at the array of clothing hanging there. "Where did all this come from?"

"I saw that you possessed only a minimal amount of

belongings and decided to update your wardrobe. Since you like dresses, I decided to stay in that design. They should all fit perfectly. Hunter didn't bring me any details of your mother when he gathered your information. It was you I wanted to learn about."

She frowned at the clothes. Some were elegant, some casual and she wasn't too sure if she was pleased or annoyed. Draco was definitely feeling generous. Shrugging it off, she decided on a sundress in deep red with thin spaghetti straps. It was a bit low in the front, not something she was used to wearing...or rather, something Joanne was not used to wearing. Out with the old, in with the new, she decided as she laid the dress on the bed.

"True, but you had details of my life after birth. My parents' names, siblings, and so forth. Why not my birth mother?" She slipped into a pair of white silk panties, which weren't hers either, and chose not to wear a bra. It felt liberating.

Draco paused abruptly, angled his head to her, and left the room.

"Where are you going?" she asked, hurriedly pulling the dress over her head. Draco had been right. It did fit perfectly. As she stepped into her sitting room, Hunter appeared out of nowhere.

"You called, sir?"

"When you did the research on Missy, did you find anything on her birth mother?"

Hunter shifted his gaze from Draco to Missy before responding. "I didn't think you would want to know about her birth mother. I assumed you wanted her current information."

"It's okay, Hunter," Missy reassured him. She could sense his fear and didn't much care that he was afraid of Draco, or that Draco had instilled such fear in him. "You're not in trouble."

Draco cleared his throat. "I would like you to return to the hall of records and gather whatever information you have on Missy's birth mother, promptly."

"Yes, sir." Hunter bowed.

"Why don't we do it?"

"Pardon me?"

She smiled at Hunter as she stepped in front of Draco. "Why does Hunter have to do it when we could do it just as easily?"

"It's his job."

"I know, but...I think I would like to look into it myself. No offense, Hunter." She angled her head to him, pursed her lips.

"None taken, miss."

"All right, if you insist. You may go, Hunter."

"Yes, sir. Is there anything else I can do for you?"

Draco shook his head. "Nothing for now."

"You make him too tense," Missy informed Draco after Hunter left.

"A tense employee is a diligent employee."

"Of course they're diligent. They fear you'll kill them if they're not. You really need to lighten up on him." She walked back to her room to grab her hairbrush and as she turned, saw the scowl on his face. "Don't pout, Draco. It's unbecoming of your villainous persona."

He scowled at her as he lit up a cigarette. "Demons don't pout. But to please you, I'll lighten up on my employees."

She smiled knowingly. "Take a look in the mirror, Draco, and tell me demons don't pout." Patting his cheek, she snickered. "Think we could get on with the search now?"

He turned his face away and drew on his cigarette. "By all means." He waved his hand at her and scowled. *Does she have to change me all at once?*

"I'm not trying to change you, Draco, just make you ease up a little. Trust me, your employees will respect you more for it."

"They respect me just fine now." He had an ashtray appear in his hands, and flicked his ashes into it, still scowling.

"No, they fear you. Big difference. Now, where are we going?"

He waved the ashtray and cigarette away, and held out his

hand. "Allow me."

She took hold of his hand and before she could blink, they stood in a dark room surrounded by huge cabinets that reached all the way to the ceiling. "Where are we?" Given that she could see in the dark, which surprised her, there was no need for lights.

"Greensburg Hall of Records. You were born here," Draco explained while he walked along the long corridor between the cabinets.

She stopped short when he floated up in the air. Though she knew he had powers, as did she, seeing him floating above the ground was still a little startling. "How do you know where I was born?"

"Hunter found your identification in your room. It was how we were able to find out who you truly were."

"He snooped in my room?" She felt very unsettled by that.

"It's my house," he responded calmly. A long shelf slid out from the wall of cabinets.

"True, but it was my personal belongings he searched through. That's an invasion of my privacy." He floated down, holding a folder, and came to a stop in front of her.

"You want me to apologize for trying to find out about you. I won't. You weren't on the list of invited guests. For all I knew, you could have been there to cause me harm. Here. I have your mother's folder."

She pursed her lips. He had some logic in his explanation, still...When he began to walk away, she hurried after him. "Now what do we do?"

"We look into who your mother was. Ah, there is a table."

She followed him to the small steel table off to the side of the room. There was only one chair and before she could mention it, Draco had another appear alongside. She took it, sat, and waited while he opened the file. "What if someone sees us?"

"We'll vanish before they have a chance to find us. Well, this is interesting."

"What?" She slid her chair closer to his so she could see the folder better.

"Your mother was apparently Wiccan."

"What's that?" She leaned in closer to read the small typed letters on the paper.

"Wiccan? It's a religion involving witches."

"My mother was a witch?" She had no idea there were still witches.

"Apparently. Here is her birth certificate."

Missy took the paper copy of the certificate and held it up to read. Her birth mother had been born in California to a single mother, father unknown. They had that in common, and when Draco pulled up her death certificate, she realized other similarities. "She was barely older than me when she died." It surprised her to read how young her mother was when she died.

"So young," Draco sighed.

"And she had no family. According to this, her mother passed away several years after Michelle was born." How sad was that, Missy thought as she read on. "It says here she was taken in by a Lily Moseby. I wonder if she's still alive?" She spun around at the sound of a drawer opening behind her and saw a folder float toward them. "What's that?"

"Lily Moseby's file." It landed on the table before them. Draco flipped it open, passed by her birth certificate and stopped when it came to the census report. "Born and raised in Greensburg. I have her home address and her place of employment."

"I can't believe how much information is in these files."

"The government believes in keeping track of everyone. Would you like to take a trip to see her?"

"Who?" She flipped through the pages of her mother's information and stopped when she saw the image.

"Lily Moseby." He leaned over her shoulder. "My, that is a stunning picture. You could be your mother's twin."

Missy couldn't agree more. Her mother not only had long

black hair like her own, but their facial features were almost identical, right down to the golden eyes. "She has my eye color."

"I've never known anyone with that eye color."

Neither had Missy, and she wondered why she and her mother had it. "I think I would like to see this Lily Moseby."

The files closed and disappeared as Draco got to his feet. He held out his hand. "Shall we?"

With a deep breath, she stood. Linking her hand to his, she was transported to an alley. "I always feel a little disoriented when you do that." Even now her head was buzzing.

"Probably the human in you. Your system will adjust. It's best, you know, not to do that to a human. It plays havoc with their systems."

"What happens if you transport a human?"

"Best case scenario, they end up feeling as if they've been turned inside out."

"And what's the worst case scenario?"

"You actually do turn them inside out."

She stared at him a moment before responding. "Well." She took a deep breath. "What are we doing here?"

"This is the home of Lily Moseby." He took her hand and led her around to the front door. He lifted his hand to knock, but she stopped him. "What's the problem?"

"I...uh...think she's occupied." She heard it as clearly as if she were in the room with the couple. Panting, grunting, bed springs squeaking, bodies slapping together.

Slowly, his lips curved up in a grin. "You can hear the occupants engaging in sexual activity and it makes you nervous."

"Yes, and you can wipe that grin off your face." So what if hearing someone else during sex bothered her?

"It's cute. It's a shame to interrupt them, but..." He rang the bell once, twice, before lowering his hand. "They're not happy, I take it."

"That's an understatement. Boy, I really don't like reading

people."

"I'll help you block the thoughts." The door opened to a scrawny young man wearing only jeans, and smelling of sex.

"Can I help you?"

"We're looking for Lily Moseby," Draco replied.

The boy ran his hand through his messy hair. "My mom's at work. Who are you?"

"Old friends. Sorry to have bothered you." He stepped down from the door. Missy followed him.

"Now what?"

"We go to the place where Lily works."

"He couldn't have been more than sixteen."

"Most likely."

"And he was having sex!"

He took her hand in his, glanced down at her with a grin. "The perfect age for discovery."

"That's too young to be having sex."

"How old were you when you first engaged in sexual activity?"

"Nineteen."

He stopped her. "That's quite a long time to wait."

"I always believed in saving myself for the man I intended to marry." She hadn't thought of Ronald in a good while and didn't care to think of him now.

"Ronald was your first?"

"Yes." She started them walking again, hoping that was the end of the conversation.

"That means I am your second. You've only had two sexual partners?"

"Yes, so?"

He stopped her again, drew her to her toes, and smiled as he lowered his lips to hers. Her head was spinning by the time he released her. "I find that very endearing. Well, here we are." He pushed through the door to a quaint coffee shop. It wasn't small by any means but it was mostly empty at the moment. Like your typical small town coffee shop, it had red-and-white checked tablecloths, and ordinary steel-framed chairs dressed in navy cloth. Soft music played in the background and as they walked up to the front of the restaurant, a stout woman in what Missy would guess would be her late thirties approached them.

"Table for two?"

"No, thank you. I wonder if you could tell us if Lily is working."

"She is. And you are?"

"An old friend of Michelle Dawson. She'll know who that is when you tell her the name."

"You lied to her," Missy whispered softly as the woman walked to the kitchen at the back of the restaurant.

"Not entirely. You're Michelle's child. Here she comes. Let me do the talking."

Lily was a robust woman with grey-brown hair swirled into a bun at the back of her head, and as she waddled toward them, her ample hips swung side-to-side.

"Sweet Goddess!" Lily exclaimed, her eyes set on Missy. "You're Michelle's girl."

"Yes, I am. How did you know?"

"Oh sweetness, you're the spitting image of her, right down to those golden eyes. And look at you now, all grown up. I never thought I would ever see you again." Her eyes slanted as she looked up at Draco. "You're not a friend of Michelle's, devil-man."

"This is Draco, and he's a friend of mine."

"I know what he is, the same kind that did your mother in. What in the Goddess are you doing with him? Your mother laid a protection spell on you so you wouldn't be found."

"A spell? I don't understand."

"She's a witch, Missy. What do you mean by a spell?" Draco inquired.

"I won't talk to the likes of you," Lily snorted, folding her arms across her full breasts.

"It's okay, Lily, he's a friend. He's been helping me. Can we sit down and talk?"

Lily narrowed grey eyes at Draco before nodding to the left. "Back of the room. How did you find her?"

"She found me," Draco explained as they took a seat in a booth at the back of the restaurant. "I would like you to explain this spell."

"Why did you go to him? Your mother did so much to protect you from his kind. Has the spell worn off?"

"I didn't know who he was until—it's a long story. I sort of stumbled upon him. What kind of spell?"

Lily leaned back in her seat, keeping her arms folded across her breasts. "I delivered you. It was a difficult birth, long labor. I wanted to get her to the hospital, but your mother refused. She knew she wouldn't survive it even if she were in better hands. She labored for hours. In the final hour before you were born, she begged me to help her protect you and so I helped her cast the spell. She didn't want you falling into the hands of the likes of him, like she had."

"She knew what my father was? She knew he was a...demon?" Missy whispered the last.

"She knew, but not until after he'd impregnated her. She was determined to get as far away from him as possible. It was her dying wish that you never be found by him, or any of his kind."

"And about the spell? How does it work?" Missy asked again.

"It's a barrier, if you will. Like an electrical fence surrounding you, cloaking you from those of his kind, if you ever came in contact with them. It was supposed to block your mind as well, so you couldn't be found. It's worn off though, I see."

"The electric snap we always feel when we touch," Missy said to Draco.

"Yes. It still works," Draco reassured Lily. "And that explains why I can't read you."

"It wasn't powerful enough to keep you from her, though." She turned to Missy. "Child, she wouldn't want you to be near him." Lily narrowed her eyes at Draco.

"He helped me bring out my hidden demon."

"No!" Lily gasped, reaching her hands out to take Missy's. "Oh, child, that's exactly what your mother was trying to prevent." She turned to Draco. "How...how did you manage it?"

"I found an ancient incantation. I've been searching for her for some time now."

"Why? So you can control her, make her one of you?" Lily snarled.

"It is her birthright."

"She was better off never knowing it."

"Wait, both of you," Missy tried to interrupt.

"We are not all alike. Just because her father was—"

"A complete bastard," Lily finished with a snarl.

"Guys." Missy tried to break them up by clapping her hands.

"If you like. Doesn't mean we all are the same."

Lily snorted. "Any spawn of Satan himself is not worth spit."

"And your Goddess is any better?" Draco spat back.

"At least she doesn't suck the souls out of innocent people."

"Hey!" Missy shouted above their voices, catching their attention. "Stop talking about me as if I wasn't even here. Lily, Draco doesn't control me. He's teaching me, and I really don't mind being a demon. Wow, I guess I'm coming to terms with it. Anyway, I'd like you to tell me more about my birth mother."

Lily spoke, though she kept a wary eye on Draco. "She was the kindest of women. Always there to help another if they were in need. She was a strong Witch, and at times, her power bettered mine, which—let me tell you—she enjoyed rubbing in. She had a wonderful sense of humor. It amazes me how much you resemble her."

"Do you have any pictures of her?"

"I do. As a matter of fact I always carry one with me." Lily paused for a moment, breathing slowly. "She was my sister." She reached into her apron pocket to retrieve her ID pouch. "As you can see, you resemble her a great deal. That was only months before she found out she was pregnant with you. You can keep that. I have more of her. If you stick around for another hour, I'd like to take you back to my house and give you something else she left for you."

"I would like that." Missy's heart tugged for a mother she never knew.

"Perhaps it would be best if you called home to be sure it's safe for you to return."

Lily turned to Draco, her brow creased. "Now, why would I do that?"

He smirked. "Your son was...well...engaged when we left your home."

She lowered her eyelids. "What do you mean, engaged?"

"He was—"

"With his girlfriend," Missy interrupted, having read his mind. His explanation was about to be a bit too vulgar.

"That little—oh, he is in a heap-load of trouble."

"We'll meet you back here in an hour." Missy smiled sweetly as they left the restaurant. "I can't believe you were going to tell her that her son was having sex with his girlfriend!"

"It's what they were doing."

"Yes, but as a mother, she didn't need to know that."

"Why not?"

Missy shook her head. "It's just not something a mother wants to know her child is doing. Now what?"

"I think you need to see your mother."

He'd baffled her with his comment, until he led her to a graveyard near the end of the town. When she saw the headstone of the woman who gave birth and life to her, Missy felt an ache in her chest that she knew was grief. It seemed silly to grieve for a woman she never knew, but she felt it all the same.

"She was so young, not much older than I am now." Missy wondered what her life would have been like had her natural mother lived. Would she trade what she'd had with her adopted family? Never. But she still wondered.

"Your father liked them young."

She angled her head to Draco with question. "You really didn't like him, did you?"

"I was sent to collect souls for the dark prince and I did. What I did to some of my victims—well, let's just say I wasn't very nice. But your father, he didn't give a damn about collecting souls. He just liked to have his way, at any cost. To be honest, I'm surprised he left her whole when he was through with her."

"What do you mean by that?"

"I shouldn't have mentioned anything about him. This time is for your mother. I'll give you a moment with her." He stepped away, leaving her alone.

Frowning, Missy knelt down to where her mother lay at rest, not sure what she was to do or say. "Hi." She cleared her throat. "I feel a little awkward sitting here. I had a good life," she reassured her mother, and felt silly for it. "My parents treated me like one of their own and my siblings were great. I'm sorry you died," Missy sighed, closing her eyes and placing her hand on the grassy ground beneath her.

The rush of warmth that swept into her was like a comforting hug, and made her smile. Opening her eyes, she placed a kiss to her palm, and laid it back down onto the ground. She stood, knowing that the sentiment had been received as equally as the one her mother had sent to her.

"Thank you." Draco turned to her when she joined him. "I needed that."

"I thought as much. Shall we?"

"I kept everything she'd gathered for you. It might seem silly, but I felt closer to her having it, and closer to you. And, I wished that maybe, someday, you and I would meet again."

Missy sat on the floor in Lily's living room with a large box placed before her. The tiny clothing inside smelled fresh as if they'd just been washed. She spotted a knitted blanket that drew her curiosity. Pulling it out, she felt the incredible softness of the yarn.

"Your mother made that for you. She loved to knit things and did so for all new babies born in the town. I thought of leaving it with you when I handed you to the authorities, but I couldn't part with it. I think I kept it wishing someday you'd have it, in any case. You had a good life?"

"I had a wonderful life. My family loved me with all their hearts."

Lilly nodded. "I couldn't keep you. I wish I had, but there was no possible way I could. Your...father...I would have been the obvious place to look. I wish I had kept you, to protect you from him." Lily glared at Draco.

"He's been very kind to me, Lily. More so than my fiancé ever was."

"You were engaged?"

"The human in me once was. I'm a different person now and what was in my past is just that." Missy stood, holding her hand out to Lily. "Thank you so much for all of this."

"Oh child, it's my pleasure. I don't want just your hand." Taking Missy in her arms, she gave her a huge hug. "If you ever need anything, please, feel free to call me." She leaned in and whispered against Missy's ear. "Don't let him make you into one of them."

"Thank you again, Lily," Missy said after she'd been released, not sure how to respond to the comment. "I will definitely stay in touch."

CHAPTER NINETEEN

For nearly an hour after leaving Lily's, Missy sat in her suite, holding the tiny baby blanket in her hand. Her mother, birth mother, had made this for her. The woman had loved her once and that warmed her heart. When Draco walked into her room, carrying a tray of food, she realized it had been some time since she'd last eaten.

"You said something at the graveyard that I'd like to discuss."

He set the tray on the coffee table, lifted one plate off and handed it to her. "Oh, what was that?"

"You stated you were surprised my father left my mother whole. What did you mean?" She cut into her steak, and sighed at the sight of blood and juices as she lifted the bite to her mouth.

"I'd hoped you'd forgotten about that." He cut into his own steak and ate without answering her.

"I haven't. What did you mean?"

He sighed, swallowed. "It was rare for him to ever leave his conquests breathing when he was finished with them."

The fork paused at her mouth. "He killed everyone he slept with?"

157

"He enjoyed the kill. What I can't figure out is how your mother slipped under Satan's radar."

She finished chewing what was in her mouth. "I don't understand."

He set his fork down on the plate as he spoke. "Why are you so interested in knowing about him?"

"Because he created me. I'd like to know if I have any part of him in me."

"You are nothing like him, trust me on that one."

She hoped he was right about that. "Tell me what you meant."

He sighed, set his plate on the coffee table, and stood up. He walked to the bar as she explained. "The instant Lucifer found out a child had been created by a demon and human, he set out to find her. His goal was to terminate both mother and child, but he'd been unable to find her. I'm guessing the spell that was cast on you might have been the same spell Michelle used to hide herself."

"And she ended up dying anyway."

He came back to the sofa and handed her a glass of wine before sitting with his own. "You can't blame yourself for that."

She didn't. It just saddened her that someone so young had died. "I don't want to become like my father."

"And you won't."

"How do you know?"

He took the wine in her hand and set it, along with his, on the coffee table. "Because your heart is too pure. There is one thing, though, that I must teach you."

"Oh, what is that?" She found she wasn't hungry after all and set her plate on the coffee table with his.

"You need to learn how to deal with your demon image. How to bring it out and how to keep it locked inside."

She pulled away. Draco's image as he'd been the night he'd taken Jennifer's life sprang to her mind. "Why can't I just stay like this?" She ran her hands along her body. She much rather preferred this form.

"There are times when your true form will surface, Missy, times when you least expect it. You need to be schooled in how to control it."

She rubbed her hands on her skirt. "What's so difficult about it? I just won't let it out. I haven't yet." And she never would, that much she was certain about.

"Missy, it isn't that easy. It could slip out in the heat of anger, or passion. Or even if you become injured."

Brushing him off with a snort, she got to her feet. "We can't be hurt, Draco." He was just trying to scare her into giving in when she knew perfectly well, from her own experiences, that demons couldn't be hurt.

He turned her to face him. "Yes, Missy, we can." He placed his hand just above her heart. "A sharp steel implement inserted into your heart can kill you."

Suddenly, her knees felt weak. "I can die?" Why now did that thought bother her when only a short time ago she had been mortified that she could never die, that she would live endlessly?

"Yes, perhaps you more than I because you are part human." He ran his fingers over her cheek. "But we've strayed. We need to get back to your true form."

She pulled away again, turned to the window and wrapped her arms around her body. "No, I would rather we didn't get back to that." When had the darkness pulled in? What day was it? She'd lost track of how long it had been since she'd welcomed Draco into her heart. Since she'd become a demon.

"Why are you so reluctant to learn this?"

"I'm scared," she admitted quickly.

Draco gently laid a hand on her shoulder. "There is no need to be. Think of it as a Band-Aid. The quicker you do it, the sooner it is done."

She turned to him, her face set. "Ever had to wear a Band-Aid?"

"Well, no, but I've heard—"

"Hearing and experiencing are completely different. Trust

me, it hurts like hell no matter how fast you yank it off. That is a bald-faced lie parents tell their children so they aren't scared, but after the first experience, we know better." She remembered the many times her parents had fought with her to pull off a Band-Aid that was weeks old.

She missed her family dearly.

"All right. If it makes you feel better, I can change with you."

"No!" She held up her hand. "I prefer you like this." She didn't care to see his beast form, not now, not ever again.

"This is only a form, one that's necessary to survive in a world of disbelievers, but it isn't the real me."

"I know all too well what your true form looks like. And I would rather not look like that." She realized she was hurting him, but she wasn't going to do things she wasn't comfortable doing and showing her demon side was one of them.

"I realize when you saw me the first time that it was rather traumatic. I'm sorry for that. It was a difficult circumstance." He took her by the shoulders. "But that is who I am, and it is who you are as well."

"No." She brushed his hands from her shoulder. "I'm not like that. I can't be." Won't, not if it meant having to look like him.

"Missy, let me show you just once, how to train it. If you chose never to do it again, so be it."

No, she didn't. "I don't want to see myself. I don't want to become a monster like you." She ran from the room, slamming the door in her wake.

Draco sat at his desk, a glass of brandy in his hand, a cigarette smoldering in the ashtray beside him. His chest still hurt from Missy's words. She made him sound so monstrous, hideous, and he was anything but. She was anything but. She'd been beautiful the first time she'd let her demon form slip out.

She'd had no knowledge that it had come out during their lovemaking, but he'd seen it and he'd fallen even more in love with her. If only he could make her see how beautiful being a demon was.

Sensing Hunter's presence outside his office, Draco waved his hand, causing the door to open.

"Is there anything I can get for you, sir?"

"Nothing for now, Hunter." He lifted his glass and Hunter turned to leave. "Hunter, wait."

Pausing, Hunter turned back. "Yes, sir."

"Do you have a minute?"

"For you, sir, always." He smiled freely as he entered the room.

"Please, sit down." Draco held his hand out to the chair in front of his desk. "Would you care for a drink?"

"No thank you." He took his seat, and unbuttoned the bottom button on his trim brown suit jacket.

"What do you know about women, Hunter?" Draco looked up at the man who had been his aide and friend for decades and was grateful to have him. He wasn't always kind to him, he realized now, and felt bad for it. Missy had been right about that. It was another of her painful statements.

"I know they're temperamental, unpredictable, and cruel at times." Hunter paused to smile. "And we can't live without them."

Chuckling, Draco nodded as he crushed out his cigarette. "That is a fact." He sighed. "Missy thinks I'm hideous in my demon form and is determined not to let hers out."

"I'm sure she will come around, sir."

"I'm not sure about that." He lifted his glass and sipped.

"She just needs time to adjust."

"She's unwilling to accept who she is." He swirled the brandy in his glass, watching the ripples in the liquid, his heart aching.

"It's only been a short time for her. She was human for much longer, and she was thrust into being a demon. You were created this way. It would be the same for you if you suddenly became human."

Draco shuddered; he didn't want to think about that. "I suppose you're right." He hadn't really ever thought of it that way before.

"Do you love her?"

Draco glanced up at Hunter and let his emotions free. "With all my heart."

"Will you still love her if she chooses to live as a human?"

"Of course." It was, after all, the human that he had fallen for in the first place.

"So tell her that."

At times, his friend could be very wise. "Interesting thought."

"If I may offer some advice?" he waited, and Draco nodded. "True love means accepting the person for who they are, not what you want them to be. Her fiancé abused her, dominated her, and wanted her to conform to his will. He didn't accept her for who she was and it cost her dearly. That is a hard wound to heal. She might be afraid to give because she gave once and it nearly ended her life."

Draco had to give the guy credit. What he said made perfect sense, and he remembered Missy stating exactly that once before. Why hadn't he realized that sooner? He should have known she would be wounded from her abusive relationship, and that he'd pushed her into a corner. Was it any wonder she came up with her claws ready?

"You are a treasure, my friend. I'm not sure I would know what to do without you."

Hunters smile filled his face. "I feel the same way, sir."

"Share a drink with me, old friend?" Draco snapped his fingers and set a glass of brandy on the desk.

"Don't mind if I do." Hunter took the glass in his hand and lifted it in salute. "To the misery of love."

Laughing, Draco touched his glass to Hunter's. "I'll drink to that."

CHAPTER TWENTY

In her room, Missy sat on her bed, feeling horrible for what she'd said to Draco. He'd been nothing but kind to her and what did she give him in return? Insults. She had been downright rude to him. Sure, she found his demon image terrifying, but she should have kept that thought to herself. She could have found some other way to tell him she didn't want to bring out her demon form.

Drawing in a deep breath, Missy knew what she had to do. What exactly she was going to say to Draco she wasn't sure, only that she needed to make amends. She needed to apologize to him. She just hoped he was in a forgiving mood.

What she found stunned her.

Sitting on the floor in his office, leaning sloppily against the wall, Draco and Hunter sang some sort of song, badly out of tune. Draco held a bottle of bourbon in one hand, and braced his body upright with the other. His shirt was unbuttoned to mid-chest, tugged free of his pants. His hair was a mess. She'd never seen his hair disheveled before. It gave him a human quality and was rather appealing.

Hunter had tossed his suit jacket. His shirt hung out of his pants and partially open. Like Draco, his hair was messed up.

Staring down at the drunken pair, she wondered what the

occasion was.

Laughing, Draco lifted his head to Missy. "I don't think I should have had that third bottle, Hunter. I'm hallucinating." He blinked a few times, his words slurred. "I'm seeing Missy."

Three bottles, good God.

Hunter lifted his heavy head to Missy, fighting to keep his eyes open. "Wow, sir, that's a powerful hallucination. I can see her too." He slurred his words as badly as Draco had.

Missy shook her head at the two. They were unbelievable. Two grown men, drunk and stupid. What a sight.

"Oh no, Hunter, look out. She's shaking her head." Draco tried to sit up, but ended up falling against Hunter instead. "Don't piss her off! She's worse than me when she's mad."

"No way, sir. You're much worse," Hunter slurred. His head wobbled when he tried looking over at Draco.

"Thank you," Draco chuckled drunkenly, lifting his bottle to Hunter's. They missed hitting each other's bottles and laughed at their clumsiness. "Hey, you want to know something else about her, she's great in—"

"Okay, boys, that's enough. The party's over." Clapping her hands, she got their attention, and not a minute too soon. If she'd let Draco finish his sentence, she was sure he would've spilled the most intimate details of their lovemaking sessions. Some things were personal.

"Holy fuck, sir. Your hallucination speaks," Hunter stammered as he grabbed hold of Draco's arm.

"I wonder what else I can make her do?" Draco laughed, and nearly fell on his face when Hunter disappeared. "Where did he go?"

"I sent him away." Kneeling down, Missy helped Draco sit upright and shook her head. She'd never seen him like this. It was rather amusing.

"Are you going to punish me and send me to my room too, Mommy?" He broke into hysterical laughter, his drunken body leaning heavily against hers for support.

Shaking her head, she shifted him so her arm rested around

his waist and under his arm. "Okay, big boy, let's get you to bed." She sent them both to his room and set them on his bed.

"All right, some action." He groped sloppily for her only to be shoved down on the bed instead.

"Dream on, Draco." She pulled his shoes off and slid his legs under the covers, laughing softly. Apparently, she would have some time to think about what she would say to him. He was in no condition to talk now.

She sat at Draco's side for hours, watching him sleep. He truly was a beautiful man. Yet the beast he kept hidden wasn't equally so. How was she going to tell him she didn't want to be like him without hurting his feelings?

Stretching her back, she got to her feet. Placing a tiny kiss on his forehead, she left Draco to sleep off his drunken stupor. Hearing a noise coming from the kitchen, she cautiously moved toward it. She was surprised to see Hunter sitting at the table. His eyes were swollen, his hair still messy. He wore a wooly brown robe and looked like death warmed over. She took pity on him instantly.

"So you weren't a hallucination?"

"Sorry to disappoint you. I assure you I am very real." She poured them each a cup of coffee already brewing. "You look like hell, Hunter." She handed him the cup, as she took a seat across from him at the table.

"Thanks. I'm sure I feel worse."

"What was the occasion?"

"There wasn't one. Draco needed a shoulder to cry on, so to speak. I just happened to be available. The next thing I know, my head is splitting in two, my stomach's swirling and I think I must have swallowed a dozen caterpillars." He shuddered, and sipped slowly from his cup.

He really looked awful. Since she had no idea where Draco kept his pain medication, or if he even had any, she conjured up a bottle of Tylenol. Missy dumped two into her hand, and handed them to Hunter. "These should help."

Lifting his heavy head, he took the offered pills and downed them with the coffee. "Thanks."

She nodded in response. "I hurt him. I expressed some things to him that were mean." Was this where Hunter would lecture her and tell her off? She couldn't blame him if he did.

"You're both hurting. You just need to talk it out."

"Yes, we do."

"Bear with him, Missy. This is all new to him."

She twisted the cup in her hand. "It's a little new to me as well."

"Draco's never cared for someone as much as he cares for you. Even before he knew who you truly were, he cared about you. He's never felt that way for another woman, ever."

"That can't be right."

"It's completely right. Don't get me wrong, he's had women in his life, but none as precious as you. He would get his fill from the other women and send them on their way. But with you, even knowing the risks, he couldn't help himself. He's never opened himself up this much to any other woman."

She hung her head down, and looked into her cup with shame. She had a lot to make up for. "I'm surprised he didn't lash out at me for what I said to him."

"He loves you too much to do that." He sipped from his cup, his eyes peering over the rim at her.

"You've been with him a long time, haven't you, Hunter?"

"More years than I can count."

"You're very loyal. I know he hasn't always been kind to you."

"Everyone has moments of cruelty, but I owe him my life." He lifted his cup, sipping slowly.

She lifted her head. "What do you mean you owe him your life?"

"Draco found me in a gutter when I was barely in my twenties. I was near death from a lethal combination of drugs and booze. I had no family, no home, and no reason to live. He took me in, gave me a job, a reason to live, and gave me immortality. I owe him my life and will be eternally grateful for what he's done for me. But mostly, I owe him for being the best friend I ever had."

She laid her hand over his and smiled. "You're a good friend to him as well." There was so much about Draco she didn't know that she hadn't asked. She'd let her opinion of what he was cloud who he might be.

He shrugged. "He may be hard at times, but he is a good man, a loyal man. Not many people see the gentle side of Draco, but it's there. He doesn't tolerate weakness or disloyalty but he has a heart, a heart that feels pain and heartache just like everyone else. Most people see the dark side of him, but under that image is a very sensitive, caring man." Hunter smiled. "And he would no doubt spew some venom at me if he knew I had said that."

She smiled at him. She knew about Draco's sensitive side. It was in the way he'd filled her room with every flower imaginable, the way he held her, caressed her and kissed her. The way he'd taken her soaring above the clouds when she'd been blue. He was kind, and she'd been horrible to him. "I've been such a fool. I'm just scared of what I might become if I let myself become completely demon."

He gave her hand a gentle squeeze. "Go to him, tell him how you feel. You would be amazed at how understanding he can be."

"Thanks for the little pep talk, Hunter. I needed it." She placed a hand on his and cured him of his hangover.

"Oh, what a relief! For that I would bow at your feet."

"I would rather you didn't." She laughed as she stood. Now came the hard part, asking for forgiveness.

Taking the stairs slowly, her mind working, Missy tried to figure out just the right words to say to Draco. She would tell him how afraid she was of becoming something vile and hideous, a monster. She had to be honest, but without hurting him. Mostly, she knew she had to let him help her bring out the demon inside of her. Draco was right. She could have him help her draw it out, learn how to control it, and never bring it out again. Reaching the top of the stairs, she turned to Draco's suite, drew in a deep breath, and stepped into the room. She found him sitting on his bed. His head hung down, his face in his palms.

She took another deep breath, and moved forward.

"Feeling awful, I take it?"

He lifted his head and those dark eyes of his looked puffy and tired. "Awful is too mild a term for what I feel at the moment." He ran his fingers through his hair, smoothing it somewhat into place. "I'm sorry you had to see me like that."

"I'm not," her voice was soft as she stepped up to him. "You looked cute when you were drunk."

"I don't think anyone has ever called me that and lived to tell the tale. Holy hell, my head hurts."

Leaning down, she kissed his pain away. "Better?"

"Much." He drew in a breath before speaking. "So..."

She cleared her throat and went for it. "I'm sorry for what I said to you, for my hurtful words."

Taking her hands in his, he brought them to his lips, and caressed her knuckles with a kiss. "You're forgiven."

"I didn't mean to be hurtful, it's just...well, I'm scared of becoming a monster."

"You could never become a monster, Missy. Your heart is too kind."

She hoped he was right. "Okay, I'm ready for you to teach me how to keep my demon from surfacing."

Standing, he took her into his arms. He leaned down, and kissed her full and hard on the lips. "I feel so much better now."

"You smell like a brewery." She waved her hand at him, laughing. In a blink of an eye his hair smoothed into place, he wore a black shirt and silver tie, and smelled like heaven. "Better?"

"Much." She stepped back and sighed. "Okay."

"Okay." He led her out into the sitting area. "Take a few deep breaths to relax. Draw in deep within and let out the frustration." He inhaled, holding it for several seconds before slowly releasing it.

Mimicking him, Missy pulled in some air, held it, released it slowly.

"Good, now go deep inside, past the human part of you, way down to the darker side."

"No." Her eyes shot open. She would never go to the darker side of herself.

He took her hands in his and began stroking her knuckles with his thumbs. "Relax, Missy. It isn't so bad."

"Easy for you to say."

With one quick tug, he pulled her against him and captured her mouth in a mind-blowing kiss. While his lips nipped, his tongue probed and his hands soothed her. And just as quickly as he captured her mouth, he released her. "Better."

"No, now I just feel...never mind." She waved it off with a smile. "Let's get this over with."

"Okay, close your eyes and go inside."

"I'm inside. I know, go to the dark side."

"Can you see it, the darkness?"

"Yes." She tensed up as she stepped away from what was human to the part that was darker, more dangerous. It was cold, so cold there, and lonely.

He gave her hands a reassuring squeeze. "Embrace it, Missy. Don't fear it."

She tried, but it was so dark, so dangerous.

"I'm here, my love. I won't let anything happen to you." He stroked her arms in reassurance and she began to relax.

He'd never called her that before, my love, and it warmed her heart. She took comfort in that and in his hands, the way they soothed her, made her feel safe. Slowly, she took a step closer. "Okay, I'm there."

"Good, now let it surround you."

She was hesitant to do as he asked. It bothered her that she had such darkness inside of her, but she was determined not to let it consume her. "Done."

"Good. Now, open your eyes, Missy, and hold on to it."

She saw him, the moment she opened her eyes, and gasped. He'd changed. Filled with fear, she jumped back and away. The memory of what he'd done flooded her.

"Missy—"

"No." She held up her hand when he reached out to her. "No, don't." Spinning around, she dashed from the room, fear filling every part of her, tears clouding her eyes.

She ran and didn't stop until she was safely in her room and the door shut securely behind her. He hadn't followed her. For that she was ever grateful.

The tears she shed slid down her face like hot buckets of water but she was too afraid to wipe them away, for fear of touching her face. Turning, she caught her reflection in the mirror and cringed. Through foggy eyes she saw, and found no need to scream.

Stepping closer, Missy tilted the mirror so she could see better. She stared back at herself with deep red pupils. How odd, she thought, that she should look so normal with that color. There were definite changes, and surprisingly, not grotesque ones. Carefully she lifted her hand to feel the skin that had now become a deeper bronze. Her eyes drifted to her hands, the longer fingers, and longer, sharper nails. When she touched her face, she found it warm, and it was soft, not at all what she had expected. There were faint ridges on her face, but when she touched them, her skin felt no different.

Stepping back, Missy took in the full length of herself in the mirror and let out a deep, relieved breath. It wasn't so bad. Missy knew that behind all the changes still lay the same woman she'd been an hour ago, a week ago, a year ago. She may not be human any longer, but she was still the same person she'd always been. She wasn't a monster. Appearances were definitely deceiving.

Suddenly it hit her, hard. Hadn't she judged Draco on appearances alone? She'd pegged him a vile, hideous bloodthirsty monster, when in the time she'd been with him, she had yet to see him as that. Instead, he'd been attentive, kind, gentle. Not a monster, not a beast. A man.

Yes, he was a demon, but below that was so much more. Hadn't he taken her on a wonderful ride high in the sky when she'd been blue, just to lift her spirits? Yes, he had. And when he made love to her, was he not gentle and caring? Always.

So much had changed since she'd left Ronald. Joanne Morrow had died, giving way to Missy Green. Now Missy Green was a demon-slash-witch. As much as she wanted to be normal again, she knew she couldn't be. This was reality. She was a demon. Draco was a demon. It was time she learned to accept that.

Sighing, she ran her gaze over her form. She would accept it, parts of it, but not all. She would never kill. She was as certain of that as she was that she stood now. And she would never bring her true form out again. She would be as she'd been born. A human. The demon inside would stay hidden.

Staring at herself, she suddenly realized she had no idea how to pull the form back inside. She had run before Draco could explain it to her, and now, she needed him to help her draw it back in.

With her head held high, Missy left her room. Again, she'd hurt Draco, and again she was about to ask his forgiveness.

CHAPTER TWENTY-ONE

Missy entered Draco's office to find him standing by the terrace windows, still in his demon form. He looked sad, she thought, as he stood looking out, and she knew it was her fault he felt that way. She hadn't been the most kind. But as she watched him, she realized one thing: he wasn't that scary now. If anything, he looked vulnerable. If she hadn't been able to pick up on his thoughts, his feelings, she would still know how he felt. It was written all over him, in the way he stood, the way his face looked so somber.

And she knew he knew she was there, waiting for her to make the first move. So she did.

"I'm trying to accept this, Draco. You, me, what I've become, but I...it's not an easy task." Some apology, she sighed, but remained where she was.

"It will get easier with time." He remained as he was, looking out through the glass.

"Maybe it will." She let out another sigh and dropped her shoulders. "Can I ask you something?"

"Of course."

It was a tough question. One she needed to know. She wet her lips nervously. "What is it like, killing?"

"I don't think you really want to know that."

"I need to know." To understand.

"Can I turn around?"

She was taken aback by the emotion, by the sweetness of his question. No, this was no hideous beast. This was a kind, caring man. "Yes."

Slowly, he turned to face her. She didn't gasp or become repulsed by him this time. "Killing, feeding off of flesh, is a high no one can know unless it is experienced. It is greater than you, overwhelming, overpowering," he explained in a calm voice. "And if you let it, it can become addicting."

Well, she certainly didn't have to worry about becoming addicted, considering she never planned on feeding off of flesh or drinking blood. "Do you...kill often?" she blurted out.

He kept his eyes focused on hers. "Not as often as I once did. When I was collecting souls, I had a quota to fill, but once I fulfilled my duties to Satan, I stopped. Well, for the most part." Producing a cigarette, he lifted his hand to his mouth and drew in a long drag. The cigarette looked so small between his large, clawed fingers.

"Why?"

He angled his head. "Why did I stop?"

"Yes. After your duties to Satan were done."

Letting the smoke linger in his mouth, he replied, "I wanted more. I'd started Starr Industries in my last years working for Satan and I'd grown very successful. Being in charge, collecting properties, running businesses gave me more of a thrill than taking a life."

She twisted her fingers nervously. "Do you still need flesh and blood?"

He waved his cigarette away. "I find it in other ways, animals mostly. Hunter usually keeps the cooler stocked with fresh animal blood. I've been off human blood for so long that tasting it now is like...well like an alcoholic going years without a drink, and giving in and having drink. It's a struggle to not cave into my craving."

"I don't want that. Drinking blood, tasting flesh," she

clarified.

"There will come a time, Missy, when your craving for blood will be too great to ignore."

"It hasn't yet. Maybe it never will." She had to believe that, even the thought of devouring a human repulsed her. She could never sink her teeth into flesh.

"You are eating your meat more raw these days, am I correct?"

She paused, looked down. "Yes." Though she preferred not to think of it, she knew she was.

"And each time you eat, a small part of you still feels unsatisfied, correct?"

She sighed. "Yes." It was hard to swallow the truth sometimes.

He took a step closer. "It is only a matter of time before you will be overcome with the desire to feed."

Her gaze came up to his. He looked so different in his demon form, yet still so utterly handsome. "Maybe because I'm more human, I won't." She so desperately wanted to believe that.

"Perhaps. Is that something you want to chance?"

She shook her head.

"There are ways to attain blood without feeding off of the living. I have mine in wine. That's why I mostly drink red."

"I guess I could do that, if the need became too strong." She'd never been a drinker, even in her youth. Living with Ronald and seeing what alcohol did to a person, she'd been determined never to touch the stuff. But she supposed a glass of red wine a day wouldn't be that bad. "I saw myself, in the mirror."

"Not so bad, is it?"

Her lips curved up in a sly grin. "No."

"You haven't changed back yet?"

"I, uh, didn't know how." She blushed.

His eyes glittered with amusement as he smiled. "You need my help?"

It was odd how suddenly seeing his jagged teeth didn't repulse her. "If you wouldn't mind, I would appreciate it if you showed me how."

"I could, but first I would like something from you?"

"Okay, what?" she asked hesitantly.

"Can I touch you?"

Again his sweetness overwhelmed her. Smiling, she responded, "Yes."

Slowly, his hand rose to her face. His fingers skimmed over her cheek, along her chin, and with a single finger, lifted her face. "You are absolutely beautiful, Missy."

Her eyes filled with tears. It wasn't just the words. It was how he looked at her. With one look, she felt the way he saw her, beautiful. "I feel so awkward like this."

Taking her gently by the arms, he drew her to him. "You'll get used to it, in time." He slid his fingers through her long ebony hair. "I need you, like this."

"I don't know—"

"I won't hurt you, Missy."

No, she knew he wouldn't. His thoughts were too pure. "I know."

He took her face in his hands and brought their lips together.

She felt as if it were her first time with a man, and in a sense, it was. She'd never been with a man in demon form before. Her body was both tense and acutely aware of its needs. She wasn't sure how to act, what to do, how to please him in this form.

When his long fingers slid over her, she quivered. When his nails scraped her skin, she shook with excitement. She had a vague recollection of having felt this before, but he was clogging her brain with so many sensations, she found it hard to think straight.

He touched her with clawed hands, which caressed her with gentleness despite their dangerous look. His lips teased desire out of her as they stroked her neck. Her body came alive with each touch, with every kiss, and pushed all fear she'd felt earlier away. Looking into his eyes, she was awash with emotion. The way he looked back at her made her feel like she was the only woman in the world. He was truly beautiful in his beast form.

Sending them to his bedroom, he continued to arouse her with gentle caresses and warm kisses. He stripped her clothing away with such precision that it amazed her just how delicate his clawed fingers could be. While he undressed her, she sought to please him. His skin felt no different from that of his human form. His chest was still firm, his muscles tight. She knew they both could very easily wish their clothing away, but the slow disrobing drew out more sensations and brought them both to higher fulfillment.

Naked, they explored their bodies, hands touching, caressing, investigating. He kissed, caressed and nibbled. She teased with her tongue, easing her teeth over bare flesh until he was more than ready for her to sample. As he pressed her down onto the bed, she opened for him, welcoming an end to the craving he'd instilled upon her body.

He was so hard and large. As he penetrated, her loins spread eagerly for him. His gaze locked on hers as he rocked inside, one slow stroke after another. His mouth curled around her breast, suckling, nibbling, and the scrape of his teeth gave her chills and aroused her beyond control. He took each moment slowly, as if to savor every morsel. When he captured her mouth, his long tongue slipping between her lips, she wrapped her arms around his body and surrendered.

"Give me your teeth." His hands slid to her mouth. His fingers skimmed over the jagged edges of her sharp, white teeth. "Bite down, Missy. Give me your teeth."

Her mind clouded with the passion he'd brought out in her. She bared her teeth and sunk them into his fingers, and he let out a moan of delight. With his other hand, he guided her mouth to his shoulder.

"Bite."

Something primal came over her and she bit down, hard.

He shuddered. She moaned.

It shocked her when she felt his teeth penetrate her shoulder. It was suddenly washed away as her body was filled with need. Once frightened of pain, now it fueled her, aroused her beyond comprehension. As his teeth latched on to her shoulder, she bit down harder on his.

As their shared orgasm overtook them, their roars of delight shook the walls.

"You are spectacular, Missy." He slid his hands through her hair as it lay fanned over his chest. "Absolutely astounding."

"You're making me blush." Never had anyone told her so often how wonderful she was, especially not after making love. Had Ronald ever told her...no—that was over—leave it there.

"I love it when you blush. It makes you look so sweet and innocent." He stroked her back and she arched, almost like a cat being stroked by its owner.

Lifting her head, she grinned slyly. "We both know differently." She hadn't been innocent for a long time now. "I just realized something." She rested her head on his chest once more. "You know quite a bit about me, yet I know very little about you."

Playing with her hair he responded, "What would you like to know?"

"Were you ever...human?"

"I was born from the belly of a beast and raised in the pits of Hell," he replied matter-of-factly.

She stayed silent, not sure how to respond to that. Some part of her wanted to believe there was even just the tiniest mote of human inside.

"Does that bother you?"

"It's a little unsettling, but I'll get used to it." Her hand stroked his chest lightly, while her mind worked restlessly. He felt human, looked human, and for the most part, she was human as well. Or at least she had been, once. "I'll never lead a normal life again, will I?"

He pulled her up so he could look into her face. "Sure you will. Just carefully."

"I can't go to my family. I couldn't bear to lie to them and not tell them the truth." What would they even think of her if she did tell them? She shuddered to think of them despising her, fearing her.

"They are better off not knowing." He stroked her face gently, sympathy filling his face.

"I love them, Draco. To never see them again, to not be able to say goodbye...it's just so hard." They'd taken her in as an infant and made her their own. They had given her unconditional love and to never be able to see them again was agonizing.

Pulling her up into his arms, he spoke lightly. "Would they accept it if you went to them and told them you couldn't see them anymore?"

"No, no, they would search for me." She knew that for certain. They wouldn't give up until they found her.

"It's best to make a clean cut."

Her jaw clenched and she pulled away. "You make it sound so easy. This is my family, people that took me in, raised me as one of their own. I can't hurt them."

"I can't begin to understand how you feel. I realize this is very hard for you. For that I am sorry."

"Do you have parents? Siblings?"

He stroked her hair from her face. "It's not like that for beasts born in Hell. Children don't know who their parents are. We're raised by one caregiver and taught everything we need to know."

How sad was that, and how lonely. "You have no idea what it's like to walk away from someone you've known and loved, all your life."

"I suppose that is accurate."

"What happens to me now, Draco?" Her future was so

uncertain.

He stroked the tears from her face. "You stay here, with me. We start a life, a family."

"A family?"

"You, me, children. Our own family." He smiled as he wiped her face dry.

"I can conceive?"

Chuckling he kissed her quickly. "Yes, we can."

"How?"

A smile filled his face. "Do I need to explain the birds and bees to you?"

She frowned. "No, I do believe I know about that. I just didn't think I could...well, you know." She shrugged her shoulders.

"Yes, I know, and yes you can."

"In the normal human fashion?" She sounded so stupid, but she really had no idea.

"You still have a womb, eggs. My semen can fertilize them."

"I just thought, now that I was a demon, that...I don't know. Never mind." Now, she really did sound stupid.

He lifted her chin with two fingers. "You are still the same woman inside. Aside from the demon gene."

She sighed. "I'm sorry."

His brow wrinkled in question. "For what?"

"Being so melancholy."

He cupped her face in his hands. "Never apologize for what you feel and never cover those feelings up. Emotions are meant to be let loose." He kissed her nose. "Locking emotions inside is what makes a person ugly."

He continually surprised her. "Will you hold me, just for a bit longer?"

Pulling her into his arms, he stroked her hair. "Forever, my love. Forever."

CHAPTER TWENTY-TWO

Missy hadn't realized how much she needed the comfort of a man's arms around her until she spent night after night being held by Draco. Never had she felt safe and loved in Ronald's arms; now in Draco's, she felt just that. Those two words, safe and Draco, would never have sprung to mind when she'd first come to stay here. Definitely not after what she'd witnessed him do. But now, now she knew differently.

She could see a future with him at her side, a long, happy future.

Yet the past still haunted her. It wasn't just Ronald, it was her family. She missed them, dearly, and she knew she could never be with them again. But Draco was wrong; she couldn't make it a clean cut. To have her family worrying about her, wondering why they hadn't heard from her for years and years...well it was almost too much for her to bear.

Unable to conceive after a difficult delivery with her last pregnancy, yet wanting another child, Missy's mother had suggested they adopt. These people had taken her into their homes, welcomed a child that was not of their blood and made her one of their own. They gave her love, a home, a family, and comforted her when she'd been sick or upset. They'd guided her through the trials of the teen years, grudgingly supported her when she'd announced her engagement.

She needed to talk to at least one of them, and try to explain. Who was she kidding? She couldn't explain it. But still, she needed to at least say goodbye, however hard that might be.

Picking up the phone, she dialed, and hoped she could make it through without breaking down.

"Hello."

Missy shifted the phone; the sound of her sister's voice troubled her. It sounded harsh and winded. "Trisha, it's me."

"Oh, Jo, thank God you called again. We've all been so worried about you. Please tell me where you are?"

"You don't sound well, Trisha. Are you okay?"

"I'm fine now. I understand why you left him, Jo." Her sister sputtered, and began coughing violently.

She didn't like that sound one bit, or the words her sister had said. "Trisha, was he there? Did he come to see you?"

"I dealt with him, Jo. You can come home now." She coughed again.

"Trisha, you don't sound well."

"I'm *fine*. Please come home."

Her shoulders dropped. "I can't."

"Why not? We can help you, Jo. The whole family can help you. He'll never lay a hand on you again." She coughed again and the liquid sound had Missy stopping cold in her tracks.

"Did he hurt you, Trisha?" If he laid even one finger on her sister, he would pay, and pay dearly.

"Come home."

"Did he hurt you, Trisha?" Missy asked more sternly.

"I handled myself," she coughed. "He didn't stay long."

Missy needed to see her. She knew that might be a horrible mistake, but she needed to see to make sure Ronald hadn't hurt her.

With the advantage of invisibility, Missy did as Draco showed her and vanished. She just had to see, to make sure. Setting herself down in her sister's apartment, she could feel the anger emanate from the room. He had been here, and he'd left behind the stench of his rage in the air.

She saw her sister and her anger veered up. She didn't have to try to read her sister's mind to know what happened. It all came barreling toward her the moment she stepped near.

Ronald had come in, the day before, demanding she tell him where his fiancée was hiding. When Trisha explained she didn't know where Jo was, he began hitting. He hadn't let up until he'd left Trisha in a heap of bruises and broken bones. Memories of her own beatings rumbled in her stomach, making her head swirl with sickness.

Missy stood staring at her sister's bruised and battered face, and her heart was crowded with anger and hurt. This was all her fault. If she hadn't left Ronald, he never would have hurt her sister. She needed to make amends.

Whether it was right or not, Missy didn't care, but there was no way she was leaving her sister in the condition she was in.

Taking a few careful steps toward Trisha, Missy waved her hands over her sister and healed the many broken bones that filled her body. She saw the puncture wound, however tiny it was, and healed it before it claimed her sister's life. Ronald had intended to hurt Trisha, deeply, possibly even kill her. That sickened her. She scrubbed her sister of the memory of seeing Ronald. It was the least she could do.

She reached out to touch, and quickly pulled her hand back. It would be wrong to touch Trisha now. Her fate had been sealed months ago when the spell Draco cast awakened the demon inside of her. No, it was as he'd said. She needed to make a cut. A clean cut.

But there was one person she had to see, one person that needed to understand his actions drew consequences. She had a score to settle, a long overdue score. It was time to confront her past.

Moments later, she appeared in the home that had once been hers, and all she felt was misery. There was nothing happy in this house, and the anger she felt nearly overwhelmed her.

Once upon a time she'd come to this home with the high hopes any bride-to-be might have, and was quickly stripped of that fantasy. It hadn't taken Ronald long to divest her of her will or her self confidence and caused her to back down to him with fear. He'd nearly killed her.

She'd never let the anger of that rear up. Now it seemed to pollute her.

All the times he'd broken her with his cold words, his claims of her worthlessness, his demeaning her, making her feel small and pitiful, came full tilt now.

She remembered the time he'd pushed her down the stairs when she hadn't moved as fast as he'd wanted. He'd stood over her laughing while she sobbed in pain. The time he'd locked her in their room for an entire day just to show her who was in charge, simply because she had spoken up to him. And when the night had fallen, he'd taken her forcibly, just to show her he was a man.

So often she regretted showing him her pain. It only managed to fuel him more. The memory of the first time he'd cut her slammed into her. It had been an accident, at first. They'd been in the kitchen and Ronald was once again grilling her on her inept cooking skills. He'd pulled the knife from her hand and cut her deeply. She'd cried out in pain, the blood dripping from her wound. That was when he first became aroused by her pain, and took her right there on the kitchen floor. From that day on, he'd always brought a knife to bed.

There'd been times she'd thought of taking the knife, while he slept, and using it on him. But she could never quite get up the nerve. Blood and pain was not a high for her. It repulsed her. Only in the recesses of her mind did she allow the fantasy to play out. She had control and nerve and only in her thoughts was she capable of killing him.

Only in her mind.

He seduced her with sweetness and romance and had won her heart. He was much older, four years older, and much more mature. She'd fallen for him at first glance, and in no time he'd convinced her to marry him. She realized now that the controlling began from the very start. He'd been so sweet, so innocent, caring and loving and she'd fallen for him hook, line, and sinker.

When he'd convinced her moving away was for the best, she'd agreed. Missy knew now it was all part of his plan to control her. Why hadn't she noticed it before? Why hadn't she seen what he was doing? Love was blind and she most definitely had been struck sightless.

Missy hated herself for letting him do that to her, for letting him control her and for letting him beat her. She had been weak, blind, and stupid. She was stronger and smarter now, and she saw everything with perfect clarity. There was no more fear inside of her. Ronald didn't frighten her. Now it was his turn to be frightened. There was nothing he could say or do that could hurt her. She was invincible.

It was time to cut the ties to him, once and for all.

Walking through the house, Missy found him exactly where he sat most days after work: in the sitting room with a glass of rye in his hand. He looked so normal sitting there, with his face buried in the newspaper, but she knew differently. Inside he was vile and ugly.

He had always been a handsome man, and he knew it. His sunny blond hair had always been kept styled and neat. His face, dainty and soft, was nothing like the man. Maybe that was why his brutality came as such a shock to her. He'd looked so harmless. Wasn't it odd that the first man she fell in love with had looked like an angel, and the man she left him for was a demon. Draco may be a beast, but inside was a gentle caring man, so unlike Ronald.

She needed to end this part of her life. Tell Ronald she was leaving him for good, and to tell him to leave her family alone.

With a deep breath, she stepped up in front of him. "Hello, Ronald."

CHAPTER TWENTY-THREE

He stared up at her, his blue eyes wide in shock. Like a cloud covering the sun, the rage took over. "Where the hell have you been?" He stood, taller than she by several inches, but it always seemed as if he were a giant. This time, for the first time, she didn't quiver like he expected.

That shrill tone he used so often would have at one time caused her to back off. Now, she merely let it slide. "That doesn't matter. I came back to tell you I no longer want to be your wife. I'm leaving you for good."

He laughed at her in that mocking tone she knew all too well. "You're leaving me?" He grabbed a handful of her hair, as he often had, and pulled her head back. "The only thing you'll be getting is a beating for running away." He slapped her hard across the face with enough force to have her head snap back. "Stupid, bitch!" He released her hair and pushed her down hard. She landed on the floor with a thud.

She touched her face where his hand had connected. At one time, she would have wept, begged him to stop, pleaded with him, offering anything if he only would let her be. Not this time. This time she simply smiled. Her face hurt, but it was nothing compared to what it had once felt like. Now, there was only a dull ache, nothing more than an irritation. Something inside of her broke and she laughed. "You can't hurt me anymore, Ronald."

His eyes grew small and cold; his rage grew hot. Lifting his hand once more, curling his fingers tight, he crashed his fist into her nose.

The impact knocked her back, and for a moment, all she saw was stars. The next blow was from his foot to her belly. It took her breath away and she lay there, gasping.

"You're mine, bitch, and you would do well to remember that."

She could feel the anger building higher and higher in him, and his mind was filled with so many horrid thoughts, it nearly swallowed her. But before he could act on any one of his ideas, she grabbed his arm. "You've had enough now."

"Release me, bitch."

"You love that word. *Bitch*. How many times did I hear you call me that? Too many to count." Getting to her feet, still holding his arm, she confronted him. "It's over."

"I am in control here. I'll decide when it's over. " He tugged at his arm but she held on tightly. She loved the surprise on his face at her strength.

"No, you're not. I should have stood up to you long ago." With no effort at all, she pushed him and sent him stumbling backward.

He straightened himself out and looked at her with pure hatred. "I see I need to give you a lesson on who is in charge here." He marched to the kitchen and she knew perfectly well what he was thinking.

She followed him to the kitchen, determined to make him understand. "Just give it up, Ronald. I'm leaving you and there is nothing you can do about it. I want you to leave my family alone. Do you hear me?"

He turned to her, his eyes narrowed, the knife in his hand tapping against his thigh. "Oh yeah? Did your time away give you a backbone, Slow Jo?"

She sighed, wondering if she should just leave now. If it

hadn't been for what he'd done to Trisha, she would. But she had to make it clear he was to leave her family alone. "I'm stronger now. You can't hurt me." He lunged at her and even before she could react, she felt the knife pierce through her gut."

"If I can't have you, no one will."

She stumbled back, hands gripping the knife stuck in her stomach. The pain was fierce, stinging something awful and it nearly caused her to black out. Would this be it? Would Ronald finally win? She didn't want to die. She had so much to live for now. She had Draco and together they could build a life. He'd given her so much, loved her unconditionally. He was kind, gentle, and her heart swelled with love for him. Though she'd fought it, she realized now being a demon wasn't all bad.

It was that thought that had her fighting back.

The rage that filled her drowned out the pain. Lunging at Ronald, she took him down in one move. They landed on the floor with a hard thud, enough to rattle dishes in the cupboards, shake the ornaments on their stands. His hands came up to her throat and she fought him off with her own. She clawed at him, ripping flesh from bone. His screams seemed so far away. Her mouth wide—it was almost as if it happened in slow motion—she sank her teeth into his shoulder. The instant the blood touched her lips, she was lost.

"Stop! Oh, Jesus."

He tossed her aside and she lay panting on the floor. The blood coating her mouth was like ambrosia. She wanted more and as she looked up and saw Ronald before her, his shoulder bleeding, his face scratched up, all she could think was, *more*.

And that thought was what knocked her back to reality.

"You're a fucking monster."

"No, no, I'm not a monster."

"The hell you're not. What the hell are you?"

Lifting her hands, she recognized her demon form and gasped. She'd changed. When had she changed? How did she change back again? She heard Ronald running, assuming he'd flee the house and when the door slammed shut, she sat up and began to cry. What had she done? She'd let her demon out and she'd attacked Ronald. Her mind was frozen. She was clueless as how to change back, with no idea how to transport herself away.

The sound of the door opening startled her and as she turned she saw Ronald step into the room, a gun raised in his hand.

"Self defense. You attacked me. That's how I'll play it. I should have done this long ago." He cocked the gun.

"Draco! Help!" she called out. In the blink of an eye, he appeared in the room, a baffled look on his face.

"Missy?" He raced to her. "What happened to you?"

"What the hell?"

The snap of the gun as it fired startled a scream out of her and when she saw Draco jolt to the side, she knew the bullet had hit him. "Draco!"

He spun around just as Ronald raised the gun again, only this time, aimed at Missy. The gun flew out of his hand, shocking Ronald. He flew back. His body thudded as he hit the wall. Without blinking an eye, Draco snapped his neck.

Missy screamed.

"Sweet Hell! What did he do to you?" Turning his attention back to Missy, he grabbed the knife still in her gut and yanked it free.

"I'm okay." Surprisingly, the pain was gone. "Did you kill him?"

"I did. He hit you." His hand touched her face in a gentle caress. "What are you doing here?"

"I had to come back and tell him it was over. He hurt my sister looking for me. He's dead, isn't he?"

"Yes. Close your eyes."

"What? Why?" She heard it now, a deep rumble that shook the floor. "What's happening?"

"They're coming for his soul. Close your eyes."

"Draco—" He covered her mouth with a kiss. Right before

they vanished, she heard Ronald screaming. "What happened to him?" she asked the second he released her.

"The gatherers came for him, to take his soul to hell. Tell me what happened?" he asked as he examined her belly.

"I called my sister. I needed to say goodbye. I know what you said, still...I had to. She sounded terrible and I sensed something was seriously wrong with her. So I went to her. Ronald...he'd been there. He hurt her. I went to Ronald to tell him it was over between us and to leave my family alone."

"And he stabbed you, beat you. Sweet Hell, Missy, he could have killed you."

She took his hand in hers, calmed him. "He didn't. I'm fine. This will heal. You killed him."

"I had to. It was...he hurt you. I had to stop him."

She heard it in his voice even as she felt it inside of him. He'd done it for her. "I know. I'm not angry at you." If anything, she loved him more. "But I have to go back. I have to explain to the authorities—"

"No!" he stopped her with a finger to her lips. "I'll deal with it."

"Draco—"

"You've been through enough. You need to rest and let this heal. I'll get the doctor here to tend to you."

"Draco—"

"Please, Missy, don't argue with me. I nearly lost you. Can you give this to me, please?"

Relenting, she nodded and let him carry her to her bed. "I'll be back momentarily." He kissed her head before he vanished.

The events of the day played through her head like a tape stuck on repeat. She'd attacked Ronald, ripped into his flesh, tasted his blood, and had wanted more. She'd done exactly what she said she never would. She'd lost control and if she'd done it this time, odds were she would do it again.

She wasn't normal any longer and she never would be. In her cloaked invisible form, she visited each one of her family members, and did the one thing she knew would prevent them from feeling the pain of her disappearance. She wiped their minds clear of her memory. Joanne Morrow ceased to exist, to her family and to the rest of the world. She hated doing this to her family, but any other way wouldn't have worked. They would have searched for her until their dying days. This was best.

Never again would she enjoy a family meal, never again would there be gifts at Christmas, or birthdays to be shared. Never again would she feel the warmth of her father's arms around her, or the scrape of his beard when he kissed her. She wouldn't see her brothers grow old, or watch their children grow up.

There would never be any more girls' nights with her sister, eating junk food and gossiping about everything and anything. No more shared secrets, no more anything.

This was the end of her life, and her family. As the tears slid from her face, Missy sent herself soaring.

After informing the doctor to check Missy out, Draco sent himself back to the house and to the dead body. The soul had been carried away and all that remained was the shell of what had once been Ronald O'Connor. Draco knew leaving him there would only put Missy at risk of being a suspect in his murder, so he improvised. Taking the body, he sent them to the woods outside of the property and laid the body on the cold forest ground.

Stepping back, he called out to the wolves. He would let the animals have him. It was exactly what such an abusive sick-minded individual deserved. And Draco knew that at this very moment, his soul was being put through unimaginable torment. Well-deserved, in his opinion.

As the animals gathered, Draco watched while they sniffed their prey and quickly attacked.

He'd send an anonymous call to the authorities to let them

know of the body.

That should end any inquiry into Ronald's death and absolve Missy of any suspicion.

Missy set herself down in her room to find Draco pacing the floor. The instant he saw her, he rushed to her, taking her by the arms. The worry she felt wavering from him was overwhelming.

"Where have you been? I've been so worried about you."

"I had some things to clean up. I need a drink." Stepping away from him, she walked to the mini-bar and poured some sort of red liquid into a glass. She sniffed it before sipping. It went down smoothly, whatever it was.

"What do you mean, cleaning up to do?"

"I went to my family." She drank down the glass.

"Missy—"

"It's okay, Draco." She set the glass down and turned back to him. "I wiped their minds clear of me."

"You did what?"

"Don't tell me it was wrong. I already know that, but it's better they never knew of me than have to grieve for me."

He took her into his arms, holding her gently as he gazed sorrowfully into her eyes. "I'm sorry."

She knew he truly was. How strange it was to be able to not only read his mind but feel his emotions as well. Once upon a time, she thought him cold. Now, she knew better.

"What prompted this?"

"Ronald, what I did. I lost control, let my demon out."

"He attacked you."

"And what if one of my siblings argued with me? What if my father gets me angry and the demon slips out? I can't have that. I won't have my own family afraid of me."

He stroked her face with gentle fingers. "I know what you did you thought you did for their own good, and I know, even though I can't read your mind, just how agonizing that is for you. I can't tell you it will get easier because I really don't know, but I can teach you how to control your anger, how to prevent yourself from losing control."

"I think that would be a good idea. I'll miss my family and I know my heart will ache a lifetime for them, but this was the best way for everyone. If anything good has come from this, it's that I realized how much I love you. I froze up when he slammed the knife into me and I had no idea how to make myself vanish. The only thing I could think of was you, needing you."

"When I heard you call to me, felt your pull—I was so worried. I feared the worst when I saw you on the floor and I...I've never felt so strongly for anyone before in my life. And I've lived a long life."

"I know. I felt it. I feel everything you feel. It's so strange." She giggled. "I've never had a man love me the way you do. I realize that you don't want me to be something else. You just want me to be me. I wasn't accepting who I am, and that got me in trouble. I should have let you teach me more."

"There's still time. I wish, though, you'd told me of your plan to erase yourself from your family."

She read his mind so clearly and it shocked her at what she saw. "You let animals have him?"

"Don't be angry with me, Missy. I did it to protect you."

"Animals?" She backed away, letting it all sink in.

"He was already gone. It was only his body. I did it so you wouldn't be considered a suspect in his murder."

"I know." She knew his motives were pure. She felt it in every molecule of his body. And she knew it was only a body the animals devoured. But still.

"Missy..."

He'd done it to protect her. She turned to him, her face alight with a smile. "I love you."

Confusion filled his face. "You're not angry at me?"

"No." She rushed to him, laughing as she threw herself at

him. "I'm not angry at you. It just took me a moment to grasp what happened, but I'm not angry. Oh, Draco." Sinking her lips against his, she drank him in, her arms wrapped around his neck, her legs around his waist. He held her tight to his body and the emotions that rippled from him fueled her own. "I love you. I love that you want to protect me, that you want me to be a better person, that you made love to me in the clouds, that you filled my room with flowers...even though I suspect you had ulterior motives." She laughed at the blush on his face. "I love that you try so hard to be a tough guy when I know beneath all that is a heart of gold. Don't ever stop loving me."

"I never could, my love. I never could." He sent them both away, into the clouds high above the ground. As they made love, Missy found what she'd been longing for all her life.

True love.

~ABOUT THE AUTHOR~

Raised on a rural farm in Saskatchewan, Shiela Stewart relied on her vivid imagination to fill her days.

Never did she realize that her need to tell a story would someday lead to becoming a published romance author. In the fall of two thousand and six, Shiela published her very first book and hasn't stopped since.

When not writing, Shiela spends time with the love of her life, William and their three children. She has a strong affection for animals which is evident in the five cats, one dog, three turtles and ten fish she owns. Some of her passions aside from writing are drawing and painting and proudly displays her artwork in murals in her home.

Her favorite time of day is sunset and she loves to stargaze.

www.shielasbooks.ca

Twenty-one years ago a bargain was made for her existence. Twenty-one years ago was the beginning of the end.

Born to serve Satan, Aurora Starr wishes she could lead a normal life. Being a demon, that's not so easy to do. By night she takes the lives of those Satan chooses. Despite her hatred for her job, she knows she must continue, but all she wants is to live like a normal human.

Enter Scott Monroe.

Tall, blond, and gorgeous, he is more than Aurora can resist. Although mating with a human is taboo, Aurora throws caution to the wind and begins seeing Scott. But when Satan makes her choose between her family or the man she loves, Aurora has had enough.

Will love win in the end, or will Satan damn them all?

CHAPTER ONE

He screamed.

They always screamed when the shadows came to take them away, take them down. The sound reminded her of nails on a chalkboard. That guttural screech, like a cat when its tail is caught in the door, vibrated in her bones, sank into her soul, and tormented her in her sleep. She would never get used to it.

Never!

As the shadows dragged the man's soul away, she took a step back, one thoughtful step away. He had a tainted soul, and he deserved to die. Yet he was still human, even though he held other human beings in the lowest regard. He was still flesh and blood despite the fact he'd taken three lives. Now, he would be eternally damned for his sins.

Aurora couldn't help but feel remorse for what she had done. It had been she who'd taken his life away. She, the Reaper of Death.

What a burden to carry.

She longed for a hot bath, a strong drink, and a smoke. Damn it, why had she picked now to quit, when she'd just begun a new phase in her life? It wasn't as if it could kill her. That thought alone disturbed her. There were very few things that could kill her. Cigarettes weren't one of them. Why had she given them up?

Rolling her shoulders, she decided *what the hell.* Conjuring up a cigarette, she lit the tip and pulled in the rich tobacco. She smiled. Now that was much better. She indulged on the cigarette, savoring every bit she could get before she stomped it out beneath her foot. She felt much better.

Another night over, and she couldn't be happier. Taking one last look around, making sure no one would see her, she vanished into the darkness.

Aurora Starr was a demon with a conscience, and it weighed heavily on her mind. Setting herself down in her house, she drew in the familiar scents, glad to be home.

"I ran your bath and set out a nice glass of wine for you."

Hunter, once her father's loyal servant and best friend, now worked for her. He had to be as old as time, yet he didn't look it. He wore his brown hair slicked back from a rather stern, bony face. Beneath it lay a gentle man. "Bubbles?"

"Of course," She beamed then took a quick step back when he leaned in closer and sniffed. She knew damn well what he smelled, and she cursed herself for not ridding the scent of the cigarette from her clothes. "Your father won't be pleased."

"So don't tell him." Heading to the kitchen, Aurora figured her request would not be granted. "How old is this cake?"

"I purchased it just this morning."

She grabbed a plate to save herself an argument with Hunter and sat at the table to enjoy her snack. "You're going to tell him, aren't you?"

"I'm afraid so."

Without setting her eyes on him, she waved her hand and sealed his mouth shut. "Try it now."

Undaunted, Hunter pulled up a chair across from her and simply stared at her.

She continued to nibble on her cake, trying not to let Hunter's penetrating stare break her. As a child she had loved to play games on him. She just couldn't resist. He would wake in the morning to feet that belonged to a chicken. Or she would wait until he stepped into the shower, hiding by the door, and turn the water into jelly. She simply loved teasing him to see if once, just once, he would lose his cool. But he never did, and like now, he waited with complete patience. It simply infuriated her.

Snarling, she removed the seal from his mouth. "I hate when you do that."

"I know." His thin lips lifted into a sneaky smile.

She licked her fingers clean. Feeling sated, she pushed from the table. "At least let me have my bath before you tell him I slipped and had a smoke." She didn't trust the silence when he simply nodded his head.

So what if she had a bet with her father to see who could go the longest without a smoke. And so what if the loser had their powers temporarily stripped. It was worth every drag she had taken from that cigarette, and she had no regrets.

She climbed into the steaming hot bubble bath. Sliding down, she let the heated foam lull her into contentment.

Her job wasn't exactly easy. The stress alone gave her reason enough to need a cigarette. One little cigarette after a hard night's work wasn't so bad. Her father wouldn't punish her for one single cigarette. Wishing for a glass of wine laced with blood, Aurora leaned back and enjoyed the moment.

She was a grown woman after all, able to chose for herself, make decisions for herself. From the time she'd been born, her life had been mapped out for her. When she turned twenty-one, she had to do her Master's work. She hated that word, *Master*. He wasn't her Master, she was her own master. But she enjoyed life, and she loved her parents dearly, so she did as expected.

She gathered souls for Satan.

That had been the agreement between her parents and the big guy known as Lucifer. They'd be granted a child, and when old enough, that child would become his collector.

So here she was, twenty-one and under complete control of Satan. Oh, how she wanted to break free of it, if only for one day. Sighing because it would never be possible, she gulped down the last of her wine. She needed more. With a snap of her fingers, she stared at an empty glass. She tried again. Still nothing. Hunter had obviously told her father of the cigarette, which meant her father had cast the binding spell on her to prevent her from using her powers. Hunter would pay for this, one way or another.

Sulking, she slid down lower into the bubbles.

"Damn it, Daddy, I only had one."

The facility was jam-packed, as it had been for three weeks running. People were scared to go out, scared they would be next on the list, scared *it* would come after them.

It was Death.

In the past few weeks, people had begun dying unexpectedly. Heart attacks, choking, convulsions. Some said they died out of fear. Their fear came in the likes of a dark angel, a name they claimed fit the shadow that lurked in the dark, taking lives. Some said her long black hair came to her feet, similar to a cape, and helped her to fly off into the sky. Others said she had the looks of a beast cloaked in a black robe, the hood draped over her head. One look at her would be your death.

Scott Monroe didn't believe in any of it. He didn't believe that some dark cloak of death lurked about, taking lives.

There had to be a rational explanation.

Yes, people were dying—okay, lots of people were dying—but that didn't mean some dark force was involved. You take in account that these people were: junkies, derelicts, and alcoholics who had abused their bodies with chemicals. Heart attacks, seizures, and strokes were not unusual. People like that just didn't have a long life expectancy. It had simply been their time.

That's where he came in.

Owner of The Monroe Rescue, Scott took in everyone and helped to rehabilitate them. Oh, he knew what people thought of his facility, and they'd tried so many times to shut him down. But he always came through, thanks to a nice chunk of inheritance. Funding his own facility went a long way toward keeping the wolves from the door. The city couldn't pull back their funding to shut him down.

Still, there were those who tried. Saying he allowed drunks and junkies to stay hooked, that he fed their addiction, giving them a place to stay to get high. Those people had no idea how far off they were.

Yes, he welcomed junkies, alcoholics and so on, but he never, never allowed even one drop of alcohol in his place, and drugs were strictly forbidden. Each person stepping through the doors received a thorough examination for paraphernalia and hidden bottles of booze. If any were found, they were confiscated. If the person agreed to stay, they were given a bed to sleep in, a meal to fill their belly, and counseling. Some benefited from his facility. Some didn't.

Scott had come to realize over the years that you couldn't save them all. Still, he gave it everything he had. The young were what disturbed him the most. Innocent children thinking once couldn't be so bad. Once *was* bad. Worse, it could kill. But they were lured into a lie, being told it would give them so much more happiness. Instead, it gave them only pain.

He'd seen so many walk into his facility, strung-out, jittery, and begging for help. He did his best, did what he could to give them the help they needed. Unfortunately, some couldn't be helped, and it never got easier to read about, or hear that one of his people had succumbed to their addiction.

In the fifteen years since his father had opened the facility, Scott had seen a lot of misery. Too many people that had given in to the demon known as addiction. Others that had waited too long to get help, their bodies worn down by the chemical abuse. His father had been one of them.

Dustin Monroe had been addicted to cocaine and heroin.

By the time he'd agreed to get help, his body had suffered badly. Dustin wanted to prevent it from happening to others, and so he'd opened The Monroe Rescue. When his father became too weak to run the facility alone, Scott took over. Dustin had been sixty when the years of drug abuse finally claimed him, sixty when he'd taken his own life.

Scott missed his father dearly.

Once a famous rock star, Dustin Monroe had had it all. Fame, fortune, and friends. Unfortunately some of those friends had aided in his addiction. Some had not. With the help of his father's band mates, Scott continued Dustin Monroe's quest to help others fight the demon that had killed him.

Looking around the crowded facility, Scott hoped his father would be proud of him. What started out housing fifty now housed over a hundred, and some days, the place was packed. As was the case tonight.

Shutting down the lights, he listened to the quiet. Tonight they would sleep peacefully. Tomorrow would be another day.